SOPHIE'S SHIFTERS

SHIFTER MENAGE ROMANCE

ANN GIMPEL

Edited by

ANGELA KELLY

Illustrated by

FIONA JAYDE

CONTENTS

SOPHIE'S SHIFTERS

WOLF CLAN SHIFTERS, BOOK THREE

Shifter Ménage Romance
By
Ann Gimpel

One spirited woman + three coyote shifters =
e-reader ecstasy

BOOK DESCRIPTION: SOPHIE'S SHIFTERS

Late 1930s, California.

The winds of change are blowing hard as shifters gather deep in the Sierra Nevada Mountains for a war powwow. Tempers run high as they argue their next move. An unexpected attack from more Hunters than they've ever seen forces their hand, and Blake, alpha for the coyote clan, fights alongside his brothers. He's grimly pleased when every single one of their enemies is finally dead, the bodies chucked into glacial crevasses.

Sophie Laughing Wolf tracked her hated brother into the mountains. Gifted with foreseeing, she wants to make certain he ends up just as dead as he was in her vision. When the large group of men he's with are set upon by shifters, mythical dual-natured beings who can take animal forms, she hides, calling on earth power to shield her.

It doesn't work. Two shifters, back in their men's bodies, haul her from her hiding place once the battle ends and drag her before their chief. He spares her life—for now—but she senses the animosity the others have for her. They see her as a threat, a witness to multiple murders.

When the mate bond strikes, she fights its pull. So does Blake. He can't believe the gods would be so cruel as to bind him and his lieutenants to a woman with blood ties to Hunters—their ancient enemy. She runs from her fate. So does he, but the bond burns bright, transcending everything.

CHAPTER 1

*J*ed Starnes, the wolf shifter clan's alpha, made a concerted effort to unclench his jaw. He scanned the hundreds of shifters—wolf, bear, coyote, and mountain cat—assembled in a cave deep in the High Sierra and itched to shake sense into every last one of them. Gritty dust from the cave's dirt floor made his eyes feel scratchy—or maybe it was a result of three straight days of arguing. Everyone was on edge, and several shifters were engaged in a shouting match. He'd called them off earlier, but they were back at each other's throats again.

"This isn't working." Keir, clan alpha for bears, sat on Jed's right and spoke low into his ear. A tall, powerfully built man with thick, shaggy black hair and a weather-beaten face, he skewered Jed with shrewd dark eyes.

"No shit. What do you want to do about it?"

"Call a break for an hour. Send everyone outside to cool off—"

"Goddammit!" Jed lunged to his feet. Several of the men had shifted and mountain cats stood with their hackles raised, facing off against a pack of coyotes.

"Do something about your men," Keir snarled at Blake, alpha for coyotes.

Jon, alpha for mountain cats jumped in quickly. "Your pack started it," he told Blake.

"In a pig's eye they did." Blake, tall and slender, shot to his feet and raced between the snarling groups of animals. Long, blond hair was tied into a queue low on his neck, and his blue-green eyes looked deadly.

"Fuck! If he's there, I have to be too." Jon raced after Blake, screeching at his men to take their human forms. Strongly built, like the cat he turned into, his legs and arms pumped as he began throwing punches right into mountain cat snouts. His red-streaked dark hair whipped around him, and Jed imagined his dark eyes were scrunched in anger.

Jed turned to Keir, who stood next to him, a look of concern stamped into his rough features. "We can't just turn our boys loose to kill Hunters and humans."

"I know that," Keir grunted. "Yet I understand why they want to. We're all sick to death of being Hunted, persecuted, and having to hide. You got lucky finding a mate. Me too, but so many of us are alone, and they blame humans for their predicament."

"It runs deeper than the lack of mates," Jed said. "No one enjoys hiding what they are. Our people want to stand proud in the light of day. They're demanding equal rights with humans, and I can't fault them for that."

Keir tilted his chin downward. "Fancy words, wolf man. How do you propose to make something as sweeping as *equal rights* happen?"

"Jesus, but I wish I knew." Jed felt tired, like his limbs were mired in slow-setting concrete. "We need to convince humans we're not a threat. That they can coexist with us. I kept thinking this problem would sort itself out, but it's only gotten worse."

Keir slitted his eyes slyly. "We could help humans—be a resource if they'd let us. We're stronger than they are, and our senses run deeper."

"Look how well that worked in Europe during the war a few

years back. We took our animal forms to protect our allies, and they shot as many of us as they could."

Keir didn't answer with words. One hand morphed into a paw and he dragged his long, curved claws down a wall, leaving deep gouges.

Anger twisted Jed's stomach into a burning knot. He blew out a tense breath as Jon and Blake plodded back to the front of the cave. When he glanced at the shifters, he noted everyone was human again. Aggression still tainted the air, but the frantic edge had lessened.

"Fixed for now," Jon muttered.

"Yeah, but not for long," Blake cut in. "We need to come up with something everyone buys into."

"Not going to be easy." Jed spread his hands in front of him. "Not with a third of the group wanting to kill on sight. That would be suicide—"

"You think they don't know that?" Jon sputtered.

"Desperate times require desperate solutions." Blake nodded once, sharply.

"One solution is for us to simply take our animal forms and remain in them," Keir said thoughtfully. We could blend in with local animal groups, and Hunters wouldn't be able to tell which was which. They only scent us out when we're human."

"What about our mates?" Jed demanded, thinking of Alice, the tall, striking woman mated to him and his two lieutenants, Bron and Terin.

A low growl rattled from the depths of Keir's throat. "Never said it was a perfect solution. Those of us who aren't mated might agree with that strategy."

"I'm not mated," Blake said, "and I think it's badly flawed."

"How so?" Keir bristled.

The coyote shifter shook hair out of his eyes and exhaled raggedly. "Because it's giving up, saying they won, and we'll take whatever scraps the human table chucks our way."

"Fine." Keir lifted his upper lip, showing long incisors. "You come up with something."

"That's the problem in a nutshell." Jed jumped in before they started throwing punches. "If we can't agree, how can we expect our packs to?"

"I'm listening." Jon squatted on his haunches and looked up at Jed.

"We have to draft a staged approach," Jed replied. "Sort of a Plan A, Plan B, and Plan C."

"How?" Keir rumbled. "There'd have to be some pretty clear demarcations telling us when we moved from one to the other. Landmarks that would be obvious to all of us."

"Yeah." Jed crouched next to Jon. "That's always been the stumbling block. It won't help us if coyotes rampage through towns sniffing out Hunters and killing them, while the rest of us are appealing to local political leaders for amnesty."

"Do we know if the Hunters still have ties to the Church?" Blake asked. "They trained the first Hunters, but it seems to me that they wouldn't have needed the Church after that."

"No idea." Jed shook his head. "But a good question."

"Boss!" Terin and Bron skidded to a halt a few feet from Jed, breathing hard.

"Whatever this is better be important." Jed straightened. It took way more effort than it should have.

Terin raked a hand through his long auburn hair and snorted derisively. "You assigned us guard duty."

"Did you forget?" Bron arched his dark brows Jed's way.

"Yes. No. Aw, shit, just say whatever it is you interrupted us for." Jed made an impatient hand gesture. "Then you can get back to watching the mountain scenery. You have the easy job. I'd trade you in a hot second."

Keir waved Jed to silence. "They may be your men, but I bet they're not bringing welcome news."

"Hunters," Bron growled succinctly.

"Lots of them. More than I've ever seen in one place." Usually imperturbable, Terin sounded rattled.

"Define what *more* means." Jon rose to his feet in a single, fluid motion.

Blake moved closer. "How many of those bastards?"

Jed pulled himself together. "Yes. How many and how close?" Depending on what they faced, the choices he hoped they had might be pulled out from under them.

"Half a mile," Bron said.

"Between fifty and sixty. Maybe more than that. We didn't stick around to count them." Terin squeezed his eyes shut for a moment. When he opened them, fury blazed from their amber depths.

"With those numbers," Jon spoke slowly, thoughtfully. "They'd almost have to know we're up here. I've never heard of so many Hunters in one place before."

"What do you think?" Keir stood tall, squaring his shoulders and gazing right at Jed.

"Does it matter?" Jed countered.

"Yes," the bear shifter replied. "We've always governed by democratic principles, and we're not going to stop now."

Terin and Bron looked at Jed expectantly. He knew what his lieutenants wanted. They'd been champing at the bit to kill Hunters for years. He pushed his over-loaded brain into action searching for options, and it kept circling back to the same place. It wasn't that he didn't enjoy killing the sons of bitches who'd targeted them, but he feared retribution that would wipe their kind off the face of the Earth.

"Well?" Blake stared him down with eyes that had shaded to a glittering aquamarine.

"They've backed us into a corner," Jed grunted. "No way that their presence here is accidental. Not with those kinds of numbers."

"We could wipe every single one of those fuckers out." Keir set his mouth in a hard line.

"Sure we can." Jed gritted his teeth together. "I wasn't worried about us prevailing. But what happens then? Surely someone will notice when this many Hunters disappears in the Sierras. They'll send out search parties—probably for years."

Karl and Les, wolf shifters from Canada, trotted close. "Sorry, we were eavesdropping," Karl said, not looking the least bit chagrined. "Why couldn't we do what we did with that posse we killed in Canada?"

"Someone would locate this cave eventually," Jed muttered. "It's not that great a hiding place unless it has some subterranean caverns we haven't stumbled onto yet. Besides, you only hid seven bodies. It's sounding like we'll have ten times that number to dispose of."

"I wasn't thinking of using the cave," Les said. "The Palisade Glacier begins about a thousand feet above us. It's riddled with crevasses. We can dump the bodies into them. That way no one would ever find them."

Hope speared Jed with glass-bright edges so sharp, they were almost painful. There were enough shifters to not only kill, but also set up transport lines to move the dead onto the glacier. "I like it." He clapped Les on the shoulder. "It just might work."

"It will," Blake said. "So long as we don't leave blood trails."

"Clean kills," Jon cut in. "No major vessel severing. Paw swipes across the head and broken neck vertebrae."

"Should keep the bleeding to a minimum." Jed tried to tamp down the savagery boiling up from his guts. He wanted to kill and keep killing as much as any of them. He'd been trying to do what was best for his kin, but holding his aggression at bay had cost him dearly.

"Men!" Keir faced the crowd and waved his arms. "Listen up."

The dull roar of conversation quieted as better than four hundred shifters turned to face the front of the cave.

Jed joined Keir and was flanked by Jon and Blake. The others looked to him as *de facto* leader of all the clans. He wasn't certain how it had happened, but he straightened his spine and projected his voice, using magic to make certain everyone heard him.

"Somehow Hunters discovered we were meeting. I'm certain they don't have our exact location, but fifty or sixty of them are in the vicinity searching for us."

"Won't be hard," someone called from the middle of the crowd.

"No shit," another man shouted. "They'll smell us."

"Can we kill them?" a third man yelled.

A chant of, "Kill, kill, kill," rose into the air.

Jed shouted. "Quiet. Goddammit. Yes, we're killing them, but listen up. We're going to do it a certain way. Minimal blood. We don't want to leave a track a mile wide for the authorities when they turn these mountains upside down hunting for those fuckers."

"What about the bodies?" someone cried.

"Yeah, what about them?" someone else yelled. "It'd be too disgusting to have to eat them."

"Might be fun," yet another shifter muttered from the side-lines, "so long as they were still alive when we sliced into their guts with our teeth."

"What part of *no blood*, didn't you get?" Blake demanded, sounding pissed.

"Sorry, boss," the coyote shifter grumbled before quieting.

Before the room devolved into yet one more argument, Jed started talking again. "I want a hundred of you to swarm up to the glacier. Identify a few really deep crevasses, and we'll dump the bodies there. Once you've found promising crevasses, form at least two lines so we can move the bodies out of the field and onto the glacier as fast as possible."

"Decide now!" Keir thundered. "Fighters to the left, glacier workers on the right. Two minutes, men. If you haven't sorted yourselves, we'll do it for you."

"Where do you want us?" Bron spoke quietly next to Jed's ear.

"With me, but I need to determine exactly where we'll be."

Jed considered it. He'd just assumed he'd be fighting, and if he fought he wanted his lieutenants by his side, but it made sense for one of the clan leaders to oversee the glacier project. In many ways, obliterating evidence was far more critical than killing.

"I agree." Keir walked up behind Jed. "Sorry, I helped myself to your thoughts. I'll head up the glacier project."

"Excellent." Jed flashed him a grin.

"Move out." Keir bellowed and ran toward the cave's entrance, shucking clothing as he went. "Glacier detail follow me. Shift for now. Easier to travel with four feet than two. Once we get to the glacier, we'll decide if we stay in our animal forms."

As soon as he was done talking, the air around him shimmered brightly, and a shaggy, black bear stepped from the glowing light. The others in his crew followed suit, leaving in a cloud of dust raised by claws digging into the cave's soft, dirt floor.

Jed rounded up Jon and Blake. Together they faced the group. "We're going to stick with the compass points we have an affinity for," Jed informed them. Wolves will follow me, form a group, and take on Hunters approaching from the west."

"Coyotes will cover the east under my direction," Blake said.

"I'll head up mountain cats, and we'll take the southern flank," Jon told the group.

"What about bears?" a shifter asked. "What if there are Hunters from the north?"

"I know you want us with you," Bron said, "but Terin and I can lead the bears—if they'll let us."

"What do you think?" Jed addressed his question to the bear shifters.

"I'm Waldo, one of Keir's lieutenants." A tall, broad-shouldered man with ice blond hair and pale blue eyes stepped forward. "Our other lieutenant is home watching over our mate." He bowed slightly in Bron and Terin's direction. "I welcome your assistance, but I only require one of you."

"Fine." Jed looked from Bron to Terin. "Your idea. You pick who goes with our bear brothers."

"Me." Bron trotted to Waldo's side. "Ready when you are." His dark eyes glittered with bloodlust.

"I've been ready for years." Waldo clapped him on the back. "Let's roll."

Light glistened and shimmered in waves as the men found their animal forms and left the cave. Jed would've appreciated the beauty of their transformative ability if they weren't headed into a full-blown war.

To avoid a bottleneck at the cave's entrance, he let the other groups leave first. When it was down to just wolves, he instructed them to shift before herding them up the ramp that led to the cave's carefully hidden entrance deep in a huge boulder field. Hunter stench hit him dead in the face even before he was fully outside. Good thing they hadn't tarried any longer hammering out the fine points of their attack plan.

He glanced at Terin. *"Ready?"*

"More than ready." He skinned his lips back from his teeth and snarled.

The din of battle rose around them. At least it appeared they wouldn't have to chase down the Hunters. Fighting was all around them. Jed raised his mind voice so everyone could hear him. *"Pick a target. Kill cleanly. No blood. Once one is down, move to the next. Keep going until no Hunters are left."*

"What if the yellow-bellied bastards try to make a run for it?"

Jed raised his muzzle and howled with lupine laughter. *"You're faster. Chase them down. The most important thing is that none of them leave to tell anyone what happened here."*

A chorus of *"Got its,"* flooded his mind, followed by the sharp retort of a rifle blast.

"Move out now!" Jed headed for where the Hunter reek was

thickest with Terin by his side. Bullets flew fast and furious, but shifters had good recuperative powers, unless they took a direct hit to a vital organ.

A small group of Hunters shambled toward them, stumbling over car-sized boulders littering a glacial moraine from when the ice sheet above them had extended much farther east.

Watching them, Jed understood this wouldn't be any kind of contest at all. Their animal forms had far greater agility in rough terrain. *"I'll take the one on the right,"* he told Terin moments before he arced through the air, landing on the Hunter. The man's rifle clattered to the ground, useless, and Jed pounded the side of his head with a powerful paw swipe. Vertebrae cracked in the man's neck. For good measure, Jed hit the man's head from the other direction to the accompaniment of more breaking bones.

Pain flashed into his flank. Snarling, Jed glanced at another Hunter pounding him with a rifle butt. Laughing to himself at how easy this was, Jed reared up and slashed his claws across the man's eyes, blinding him before he broke his neck. He lost count of how many he killed, moving smoothly from one to another. Bloodlust warmed his gut. Sending Hunters straight to Hell was long overdue. He kicked himself for holding his men back this long, and then realized his ability to reason in his wolf form wasn't all that sharp. There'd be a price for today, but by God, every single moment was worth it.

They forced us. They came after us.

We had no choice.

Jed stopped thinking. It cut into the simple joy of dispatching his enemies. The die was cast. There may have been an alternative, but he was damned if he saw it. Hunters would've sniffed out the cave, converged on it, and murdered them if they hadn't fought back.

The occasional animal howl told him some Hunter's rifle had found its mark, but he'd expected a few casualties. He hoped no one would be mortally wounded. Losing even one more of his kin to Hunters was unacceptable.

The sun was moving toward the western horizon when he looked for his next target and couldn't locate anything left to kill. He scrambled to the top of an enormous boulder to scan the field. The sight pleased him. Not only were there no Hunters—except the ones lying on the ground—a smooth operation to move the bodies uphill was underway.

He raised his muzzle and howled. Bron and Terin sprinted to him and climbed the boulder, their claws scrambling for purchase on the slick granite. Because it would make conversation easier, Jed shifted and motioned for his lieutenants to do the same.

"Did we get them all?" he asked once he'd reclaimed his man's body.

"Yup." Bron fist-pumped the air. "Had to chase after about ten who decided they didn't like the odds, but we got them too."

"Any idea how many there were?" Jed asked.

Terin shook his head. "More than we originally thought, but less than a hundred."

"Did all of us respect the minimal blood command?"

"I think so." Bron replied.

Jed cut to the chase. "How about wounded on our side?"

"Not sure, but from where I was fighting, the few of us hit with bullets were able to heal spontaneously," Terin replied.

Jed quirked a brow at Bron. "Same question."

"Everyone knows I'm the best healer we have in all the packs, and no one called for me. That speaks for itself."

Satisfied they'd done the best they could, Jed said, "Let's round up everyone. The more of us helping, the faster we'll get the rest of those bodies out of here."

"What happens then?" Terin asked.

"We go home and lay low," Jed replied. "And hope to hell the powers that be don't launch a witch hunt to smoke us out of our homes."

"I'll rustle up everyone to help," Bron offered. He pointed at groups of shifters cavorting among the rocks, clearly celebrating their victory.

"I'll go with you," Terin said. "It'll go faster with two of us."

"See you on the glacier." Jed scrambled down from the boulder and detoured into the cave to grab his clothes. He didn't really care about them, but he needed his boots to clamber around on the icy glacier. By the time he got there, the work lines were moving the last bodies into crevasses. He inspected the glacier for blood, gratified they hadn't left very much.

As if nature was on their side, a sharp rumble blasted him moments before the cloudy sky let loose. Rain, sleet, and hail pummeled him, but he welcomed it. His hair plastered wetly against his head, and he wiped water from his eyes, but he couldn't stop smiling at their good fortune.

"Son of a bitch." Keir slid to where Jed stood. He was barefoot on the icy surface—and naked. Jed offered him points for being tough. Clearly not uncomfortable in the least, the bears' alpha was grinning like a fool. "Someone up there likes us."

"It certainly appears that way. Beyond that, you did a hell of a good job here." Jed whacked Keir on the back, and the bear shifter cuffed him back playfully.

"It was easy." Keir shrugged off the praise, but he looked pleased. "This glacier has more holes than Swiss cheese. You're the one who thought of it."

"Not me." Jed shook his head. "Les, one of my Canadian kin."

"Regardless." Keir scanned the expanse of ice above them. Water ran down his face and dripped into his eyes. "Think we're about done here."

"Yeah. Sooner we get out of here, the better."

"Boss!" Karl's voice reverberated in his head.

"I'm on the glacier. What is it?"

"Les and I were headed back to make sure we hadn't missed any bodies when we found something."

Keir furled his brows, obviously listening in. *"Whatever it is,"* he chortled, *"kill it."*

"Not sure we want to do that." Les' unmistakable inflection cut in.

"Yeah," Karl seconded. *"It's a woman."*

"What the fuck?" Jed exchanged glances with Keir, who drew his brows into a tight line, looking puzzled.

"We're in the cave," Karl said. *"We think you should come. She's mighty scared, and we need to get her out of here without her pitching a fit."*

"On my way."

Jed had turned to go when Keir clamped a hand around his upper arm. "She's a witness," he hissed. "You do get that?"

"Yeah. I read you loud and clear."

Jed trudged downhill, lost in thought. Killing a woman went against the grain, but they couldn't let her live to reveal today's carnage, either. Cutting out tongues had gone out of style in the Middle Ages, besides that would almost be worse than killing her outright.

"I'll figure it out after I get there and see her," he muttered, reluctant to let anything intrude on today's victory.

CHAPTER 2

*J*ed slipped and slid down the glacier, grateful his mate Alice wasn't there to read him the riot act. An accomplished mountaineer, she'd have laughed herself sick after the second time he fell on his ass and slid twenty feet.

"Goddammit!" Terin screeched from behind him and went flying past on his stomach. He shifted mid-slide and dug his claws into the icy surface to stop his suicidal descent. Once he'd stopped on the uphill side of a boulder, he shifted back.

Jed drew to a halt next to him. "Good thing you didn't bother getting dressed. Your clothes would be strewn over the last fifty feet of ice in shreds."

"Yes and no," Terin muttered, glancing pointedly at Jed's shoes. "My boot soles would have helped—a lot. Jesus but I'm glad Alice isn't here to see this."

"Keir's doing okay in bare feet," Bron noted, catching them up. "And I'm not doing that bad, but the soles of my feet hurt like hell —and I miss my claws."

Jed eyed the edge of the glacier. Patches of rocks and dirt, interspersed with ice, began a couple hundred feet below them. Walking would get much easier then. He grabbed one of Terin's arms. Bron seized the other one, and together they lurched over the remaining rock-studded ice.

"We have a problem," he said without preamble.

"Tell me something I don't know," Bron muttered.

"We have to get home and make sure Alice is okay," Terin added.

Jed winced. He'd wanted to leave someone home with the women, but neither Alice, nor Megan—Les and Karl's mate—would have any part of that. He reached for Alice through the mate bond, but she was too far away for him to sense anything.

"Which particular problem were you alluding to?" Bron asked. "Somehow it seems like more than getting out of these mountains with our hides intact."

"It is," Jed said tersely. "Les and Karl found a woman. They're holding her back in the cave."

Terin stopped dead. "What? Is she a climber like Alice, who got stranded up here?"

"Somehow, I don't think that's it," Jed muttered.

"We'll find out soon enough," Bron broke in. "Shit! If she came with the Hunters, we'll have to kill her."

"That already occurred to me." Jed shot a pointed look at his lieutenant. "Keir said the same. He was standing close enough to hear when Les gave me the bad news."

"Damned shame." Terin shook loose from them. "I'm good. I don't need you two to nursemaid me anymore."

They covered the remaining half mile to the cave in silence. Terin and Bron went to collect their clothes, and Jed strode briskly to a back corner where he sensed Les and Karl. Crouched behind them in a quivering mass was a woman with her head buried in her crossed arms. Long black hair shot with thick silver streaks spilled around her onto the dirt floor. She was swathed in dark colored wool and flinched away when Jed hunkered next to her.

He probed her mind and found terror so gripping, it obliterated everything else. He started to tell her not to be afraid, but the words died on his tongue. He couldn't give her any guarantees, and he wouldn't lie to her.

"Who are you?" he asked, keeping his voice gentle.

"We tried that, boss," Les said.

"At first, all she did was moan," Karl added. "She got quieter after a while, but she hasn't answered any of our questions."

"Where'd you find her?" Jed asked.

"After we lifted the last of the bodies in our sector out of the moraine, so others could move them up the mountain, Les and I sensed something living. It wasn't a Hunter, but it was human, so we dug a little."

"Didn't have to go far," Les cut in, "before we found her hiding between a huge piece of deadfall and a big rock." He shrugged. "Without our wolf senses, we'd never have discovered her."

A low whimper escaped from the woman, and Jed laid a hand on her arm. "What's your name?" he repeated.

"Just get it over with." Her low, musical voice was strained. Hysteria trod near the surface.

"Get what over with?" Jed probed. Maybe if he could get her talking, he could learn something.

The woman lifted her head from her crossed arms and Jed's eyes widened. She was absolutely stunning with huge midnight blue eyes. Pronounced bone structure and copper skin suggested Native American blood flowed through her veins. Sharp cheekbones, a hawk-bridged nose, and a squared-off chin lent her an exotic cast.

She tilted her chin at a defiant angle. "You have to kill me. I know too much. Get it over with. The others—" she cast a spurious glance Les and Karl's way "—they were waiting for you to make the decision." Her mouth worked as if she'd tasted something bitter. "Anyway, get it over with. I took my chances when I tracked my brother today. If he'd known, he'd have forbidden me to come."

Jed frowned. "One of the Hunters was your brother?"

The woman nodded mutely. "Yeah, that's what I just said, isn't it? Get it over with, white man. If you're going to kill me, do it. If not, let me go."

Bron and Terin had joined them once they'd dressed. Bron passed a hand over the woman's head, and Jed felt him probing with shifter magic. "You have white man's blood too," Bron murmured.

The woman shot him a scathing look. "Not much. What of it?"

"Where we come from in Canada," Les said, "Indians are friends to those like us."

She curled her upper lip in withering scorn. "We have enough problems without associating with shifters. You're nothing but trouble. Bad enough we got stuffed onto reservations, land no one else wanted."

Jed tried a different tack. "Why'd you track your brother today?"

She buried her head in her arms again, refusing to look at him.

"Please." He gentled his voice. "Give us something to work with. Les and Karl, my brothers who found you, didn't harm you."

"Only because they were waiting for you, their chief." Her voice was muffled.

"Goddammit!" Les squatted in front of her and yanked her head upward. "Karl and I could've killed you. We didn't. We were *not* waiting for Jed to make that call. Tell us why you were tracking your brother."

Jed heard compulsion flow beneath the other shifter's words.

The woman drew back. She tried to combat Les' spell, but the contest was laughable. "To stop him," she said. The words were clearly dredged from her, but they held the ring of truth.

"Good. He needed to be stopped," Les said. "Why'd you think he'd listen to you?"

The woman's face crumpled and she started to cry—big, noisy, gulping sobs that ripped through her. "It's not what you think. I didn't try to make him listen to me," she managed between ragged breaths. "I have the gift of prophecy—farseeing—and I knew things would go to hell for all of them today."

"Do your visions always come true?" Jed probed. Despite the problems the woman presented, her story fascinated him.

She nodded, but didn't say anything further.

"Did your brother know you followed the Hunter group?" Jed asked.

She shook her head. "No. He doesn't share my gift. His magic came mostly from the goddamned white man's Church."

"Odd none of the rest of them sensed you behind them," Karl muttered.

"Not odd at all," she shot back, choking a little on snot running down her face. "I can blend my energy into the rocks, the dirt."

"We found you," Karl pointed out.

"Because you were in your natural form, and wolves sense such things far more acutely than men."

Jed waved Karl to silence. This was going nowhere fast. Returning his attention to the woman, he said, "So you came along, but didn't talk with him. Didn't try to warn him. Help me understand why." Jed hoped things might get clearer, but so far they were just becoming more confusing.

"Let me get this straight." Bron hunkered next to Les and caught the woman's gaze with his dark one. "You saw in a vision that your brother would die, and you came along anyway but didn't try to warn him. Did you want to make certain he was dead?"

Jed silently offered his lieutenant credit for shrewdness. If the woman knew today would end in a bloodbath because she'd seen it—and she made no attempt to warn her brother—what other reason would she have had for trailing after him?

The woman's sobbing escalated. She tried to jerk her chin out of Les' grip, but he held fast. "Yes," she gasped out. "Yes. I hated that bastard. He...used me—hurt me the way men hurt women—

when I was only ten years old. He never stopped until I ran away when I was sixteen. No one believed me. No one c-cared." Her last words were almost obliterated by sobs.

Suddenly her phrase *to stop him* took on a whole new meaning. Jed just stared at her. "So it's not that you just didn't say anything today. You never planned to tell him you saw his death."

She did yank her chin away then and spat on the dirt floor. "Hell no. I haven't spoken to him in ten years."

Running on instincts that had rarely failed him, Jed glanced at the four wolf shifters ranged around him. They didn't need to talk. After hundreds of years of working together, they understood one another.

"Stand up." Jed told the woman.

"Why?"

"Did you see your own death in your vision?"

An odd look washed over her face before she shook her head and pushed herself upright. Standing she was of a height with Jed, and her hair reached past her ass. She squared slender shoulders. "Is that a backhanded way of saying I can leave?"

Jed shook his head and hurried to add words before she sank into a puddle of terror again. "You're right that we can't allow you to return to your life. We have no idea who you are, who you'd tell. We could wipe your memory of us, but you'd still recall the death that happened in this canyon."

"What are you going to do with me?" Her voice shrilled and she jerked her chin upward. "If you think you're going to abuse me like my brother, think again, white man. I'd rather be dead."

"We don't do that to women." Terin pushed into her line of vision so she had to look at him.

"Not what I've heard," she retorted. "My brother said he learned it from you."

"Bull crap!" Jed said succinctly. "I've never known a shifter to take a woman against her will. Not on my watch, and not in my clan."

"You planning to bring her home with us?" Bron quirked a dark brow.

Jed nodded. "The only question—" he focused on the woman "—is whether you come willingly, or we knock you out and carry you down the mountain."

"Home as in staying under the same roof with five men?" Her face twisted into a grimace. "No. Not happening. Just kill me here and get it over with."

"We're mated," Karl informed her. "Les and I have a mate. Her name is Megan. And Jed, Bron, and Terin are mated to Alice."

The woman tossed her head. "Fine. Just because you located some sluts who—"

Jed snaked out a hand and slapped her hard across the face. He grabbed her head between his hands and forced her to look at him. "Never say one bad word about my mate. I love her. So do Bron and Terin. Don't disparage what you don't understand."

A shocked look blossomed on her face and she muttered, "Sorry," before staring at her feet.

"Let go of her, boss." Bron pulled Jed's hands away. "She only understands what she's lived. And it hasn't been pretty."

Jed swallowed back fury. He'd defend Alice to the death if it came to it, but this woman wasn't a threat to his mate. "All right, Miss No Name." He narrowed his eyes to slits. "What'll it be? Are you coming with us willingly, or do we turn you into baggage to transport?"

"I'll come willingly." She spoke low, still not looking at him.

"It's because she doesn't trust what we'll do to her if she's unconscious." Terin wiped a disgusted look off his face.

"Doesn't matter," Jed said gruffly. "We need to leave. We've wasted too much time as it is." He turned back to the woman. "What's your name? You can either tell us, or we can dig around in your mind until we find it."

"Sophia," she said sullenly, "but everyone calls me Sophie."

Jed considered probing for a last name, but instead he asked. "Did anyone know you came up here?"

She shook her head.

"Is anyone expecting you to show up somewhere, like at a job?" Les cut in.

"Where have you been, white man?" she sneered. "No one hires Indians. Not if they have any choice."

"So no one will notice if you don't show up back on the reservation?" Les persisted.

Sophie shrugged. "Probably, but not for at least a week. Maybe not even then. Depends if the new batch of hooch is keeping everyone stinking drunk."

"Get headed down the mountain," Jed instructed the others. "I'm going to close things out here and do some last minute strategizing with the other clan leaders. I'll catch up."

"You got it, boss." Terin took one of Sophie's arms, Les the other. The group moved out of the cave.

Jed hoped to hell he hadn't made a major error in judgment. One thing he was certain of. If Sophie so much as looked cross-eyed at Alice, he'd—

Yeah, right. Alice can take care of herself in that regard.

Strong, independent, and plain-spoken, his mate wouldn't hesitate to disabuse Sophie of her misconceptions about shifters and the mate bond. Alice had thought they were a bunch of perverts too, but that was before she'd come to know and love them.

With his mouth twitching into half a smile as fondness for his mate rolled through him, Jed trotted to where the other three clan leaders stood with their heads together, deep in a discussion. The cave had mostly emptied out, and Jed assumed everyone was headed for home.

"Finally." Keir eyed him. "Sent your men out to do the deed, huh?"

"We're not killing her," Jed said, steeling himself for what had to come next.

"What the fuck?" Keir demanded. "Why not? She could sink us all."

"Hold up." Jed raised both hands. "We're not just turning her loose. We're bringing her home with us. Someone will always be around to watch her, until we figure out if we have to eliminate her."

"But why?" Blake asked. "According to Keir, she witnessed what we did."

"The safest approach," Jon cut in, "would be—"

"Goddammit." Jed punched the air with a fist. "Last I checked, we're not murderers. We killed those Hunters today because they came after us, and we didn't have a choice."

"So why'd she come with the Hunters?" Jon asked. "She'd almost have to be part of them. Women wandering by themselves in rough country almost never happens."

"Her brother was one of those we killed today," Jed said.

"All the more reason to dispatch her," Keir urged. "She'll want revenge."

"Same thing I thought," Jed countered. "Except she hated him. She followed the Hunters to make certain he died."

"Did you test her words to make certain she spoke true?" Jon asked, sounding suspicious.

Jed nodded. "Of course. She's been ill used by men, starting with her brother before she even started to bleed." Keir opened his mouth to talk, but Jed hurried on. "Hear me out. She's mostly Native American, maybe seventy-five percent, and she has magic of her own. She foresaw today's carnage and wanted to witness her brother's death. Reassure herself he couldn't hurt her anymore"

Blake's eyes widened. "A regular Amy Archer-Gilligan, eh? Woman with a taste for blood."

"I don't get that hit off her," Jed replied. "Look. Give us some time with her. Between the five of us and our mates, we'll figure out if sparing her was a mistake soon enough. If it was, we'll fix it."

"I'll hold you to it, brother." Keir stretched long arms over his head, rotating his shoulders. "What the three of us decided was we'd all show up at your place in a week and take stock of the fallout from today. That work for you?"

"Don't see why not," Jed replied. "Will you be going home in between since none of the rest of you live in California?"

"I will," Blake said, "but only because Las Vegas isn't very far away."

"I'll head home too," Keir said. "Even though it means I'll spend most of this next week driving. At least someone will see me in southern Oregon, so it will give me a rough alibi."

Jed looked at Jon, who lived in North Dakota. "What about you?"

"I'll be staying with some of my kinfolk in southern California. Their phone is…" He rattled off two letters and four digits. "Not a private line, so watch what you say."

"Got it. If I need to reach you, I'll use telepathy since you'll be close enough. I'm out of here." Jed shook hands with the other three clan leaders.

"Yeah, not much we can do until we see how big a shit storm emerges from today." Keir headed for the cave's entrance.

Jed trotted after the bears' alpha. Once he got outside, he pulled his jacket closer around him, hunching against the rain-hail mix pouring from a gunmetal sky. Luckily, gray-black clouds crowded thickly, blotting out the sun. Rain would eradicate their scent and their footprints on the glacier. When the next group of Hunters showed up to find out why their companions hadn't returned, there'd be no obvious clues. Hunters weren't like wolves. They lacked the sensitivity to track old trails, or ones that were growing cold.

He shook himself and water flew everywhere. It would make for a miserable trudge down the mountain, but the weather would be a deterrent for everybody else too. If fortune smiled on them, a big snow dump would stymie attempts to head up these mountains for months.

Whistling a tuneless song, Jed scrambled downhill. Once he hit the trail, he broke into a run. Travel as a wolf would've been faster, but he'd be naked when he got to the collection of cars and trucks parked at the trailhead, a mile above Glacier Lodge, and the last thing he wanted was to draw undue attention to himself. He hoped to hell shifters would be the only ones in the parking lot, and that Sophie wouldn't scream her head off about being kidnapped if someone else crossed their path.

It didn't sound as if she was allied with the Hunters, but she hadn't been thrilled about them dragging her home with them, either.

"Enough." Jed spoke out loud as he pelted down the trail. "I made my decision, and now I get to live with it."

CHAPTER 3

Sophie moved easily enough across the uneven, rock-strewn terrain. The men on either side of her made certain she didn't fall. Once they reached the trail, still mostly snow free because winter hadn't totally arrived yet, they positioned her between them and walked single file downhill. She eyed the territory on both sides of the trail, but making a run for it would be wasted effort. Her four escorts were wolves, and they could chase her down without any effort at all. The zing of power teased her skin, and she figured the men were communicating in some silent fashion.

Water rained down from the skies, punctuated by occasional bursts of hail. Thunder roared in the distance, and lightning bolts flashed from time to time but never very close. She pulled the thick weave of her jacket hood over her head, but her hair was already soaked and plastered against her skull.

That they hadn't killed her defied credibility. She'd been certain they'd mete out a death blow the second their chief arrived, but it hadn't happened. Not that she was anxious to throw her life away, but making certain her brother, Abe, was well and truly dead was worth a whole lot. Fury, still white-hot despite how many years it had been, started in her toes and engulfed her whenever she thought about him.

Even though she tried to stop it, a vision of his hot, sweaty, sixteen-year-old body holding her down filled her mind. He'd tied a bandana around her mouth so she couldn't scream, and he held her hands above her head while he shoved his penis up between her legs. It felt like something inside her tore into broken, jagged shards of glass. Tears streamed down her face, and she choked and gagged on the bandana, but Abe was so intent on driving himself into her, he didn't even notice. Or more likely, he didn't give a shit about anything except coming.

She hadn't known anything about sex then, but she learned fast. Damned fast.

Once he'd taken her that first time, threatening her with death if she told anyone, he showed up regularly. She'd discovered if she moved under him, he came faster, and that became her goal—until the time an unusual feeling buffeted her. She was twelve then, and her moon blood had begun to flow. Horrified by pleasure coursing through her at the hands of her brother's cock, she retreated to laying stock still and imagining she was somewhere else. Anywhere else.

He'd noticed. Hell yes, he did. He'd even had the nerve to ask what happened. Didn't she like it anymore?

She'd spat in his face and told him he was stupid if he imagined she'd ever liked him raping her. She also made it clear that if he made a baby, there'd be hell to pay. That part got through because the next time he showed up with a hard on, it was encased in a condom...

The shifter behind her, Bron with his dark hair and dark eyes, dropped a hand on her shoulder. "I'm sorry."

"Huh?" She twisted to get a look at him.

"I'm trying to figure you out, so I've been inside your mind."

Revulsion ripped through her. "Noooo. Not okay. That's just another form of rape."

Bron shook his head, and water flew in all directions. "Keep walking. It's not much farther, but you already know that. My intentions were good. Nothing like your brother. That bastard used you, and I'm sorry you had to live through that."

She opened her mouth to bite off a bitchy reply, but swallowed the words before they left her mouth. He'd actually sounded like he meant what he said.

He gave her a little push. "I did mean it. Now get moving."

"I guess asking you to respect my thoughts won't work." She plodded down the muddy trail, grateful for her stout, leather boots with their thick soles.

"I am respecting you by learning as much as I can," he countered. "Jed's a compassionate man. It's what makes him the best alpha among the four clans. He took a huge chance by letting you live. I want to make certain he doesn't end up regretting it."

"You're picking through my thoughts for him. Not because you give a shit about me." She bristled.

"No," he corrected her. "I'm doing it for both of you, but you're right that my first allegiance is to the pack."

"Hey!" rang from behind them, and Jed chugged alongside, slowing from what had been a full-on run judging from the rhythm of his footsteps. He was breathing hard. "Knew I could catch you guys. I just heard my name."

"I was telling Sophie you're kindhearted." Bron jabbed Jed in the side. "Don't make a liar out of me."

"Gawk." Jed twisted in a full circle, scanning the wet forest. "Don't ever say that where the other alphas might hear. I'd end up the laughingstock of the century."

Though she tried not to, Sophie felt the ends of her mouth curl into a smile. The men were joking with one another. It was such a foreign experience, she didn't know how to react. Men on the res were mostly working—or drunk. Not much energy left over for anything lighthearted.

Hail splattered down, harder than before. It cut into her cheeks, and she shielded her face with a hand.

"Hurry," Les yelled from up ahead. "It's going to do nothing but get worse."

The parking lot was jammed so full of cars and trucks, it took the men working together to lift two of the vehicles since there wasn't room to turn them around any other way.

Jed bent close to her. "Which one is yours? We can't leave your car here."

"I parked at the lodge behind some trees."

"All right." Terin walked up to them. "Get into the truck. We'll stop and pick up your car on our way out."

She clambered into the high cab and sat sandwiched between Terin and Bron as they started down the steep, zig zag, dirt road that led to Glacier Lodge. Les, Karl, and Jed got into a fancy looking passenger car. The hail had, indeed, worsened. It was all the truck's windshield wipers could to do keep up with it.

"Keys," Bron said, looking at her.

It took a moment to register, and then she reached into a pocket and handed him the keys to her ten-year-old Ford. "It doesn't run very well," she cautioned him. "Almost didn't make it up the hill to get here. Overheated twice, but the creek was close enough for me to pour water into the radiator."

Terin turned off the main road to the spur leading to the lodge. "Where'd you leave your car?"

She told him and noticed that Jed had followed the truck. Apparently they weren't taking any chances she might bolt. Sophie chewed on her lower lip as the truck slowed next to her rattletrap car. She should be hunting for every opportunity to flee, but she'd begun to let her guard down.

Not good. I have to escape. I can lose myself back on the res, and they'll never find me because they'd have no idea where to look.

"Bad call, sister." Bron grabbed her arm. "We have your scent, and we'd find you. No matter how far you ran."

Sophie shrank away from him. What hope did she have if her every thought was laid out in bright, living color for the shifters to sift through?

"Every hope in the world," Terin said softly. "We want to help you, not kill you. Haven't you figured that out yet? Don't make us regret our choice."

Bron jumped down. "Come on," he said to her. "Jed wants you with him, and either Les or Karl will ride with Terin. I'm going to do my best to get your car back to our house."

"Nah." Karl snapped the keys out of Bron's hand. "I'm probably a better mechanic than you, bro. I'll take her car. You can get back in the truck."

When they were done sorting who went where, Sophie found herself in the fancy, new car sitting between Jed and Les. Karl got her car going with far less fuss than she'd expected, and the three vehicles started down the road for the roadway heading to southern California.

"Just so you're not surprised," Jed's voice rumbled against her ear, "we're not driving all the way home tonight. It's too far, but I will call Alice and Megan once we're in range for my magic to reach them, and have them meet us at a midway point. Probably Mojave. That way, you'll have female companionship tonight in your motel room."

"What tribe are you from?" Les asked, following it with, "Cree live near where I used to. Many of them are shifters, just like us."

"And the Montana Blackfeet are our friends as well," Jed added. Before she could form a response, he threw more questions her way. "How old are you? How about if you tell us about yourself."

Sophie opened her mouth, then snapped it shut. No percentage she could see in laying her soul bare for these strangers.

"Tribe?" Les probed. "That's not very personal."

"Damn it! You're inside my head just like the other two."

Les shrugged. "Whatever it takes."

"Fine." She crossed her arms across her soaking wet jacket. "Just take whatever you need from me. You seem to be doing it anyway."

Jed cast a sidelong glance at her, frowning. "No. What we're doing is looking in on whatever might be going through your head. Mining for information beyond that is much harder. Not that we can't do it, but it's easier on us—and you—if you talk with us."

"Yeah," Les seconded. "Not very comfortable if we go digging around in your memories."

"Just start talking," Jed suggested. Something thick flowed beneath his words. She felt the spell—little darts of heat on her skin—but couldn't subvert it. Apparently, they had more than one way of dredging information out of her.

"Another place you might begin," Les suggested, his voice equally silky, "is your magic. No one's ever trained you to use it. Why not? Doesn't your tribe have a local shaman?"

"Sure, but he's drunk all the time." Sophie clapped a hand over her mouth.

"Start at the beginning," Jed suggested in honeyed tones. "Don't fight it."

Suddenly keeping her mouth closed with words locked in the safety of her throat was impossible. "I'm Paiute," she said. "There was a white man somewhere in the mix. It's where my blue eyes came from, but I have no idea who he was."

"See," Les crooned. "That's not so bad. We need to know about you. And then we'll tell you about us—if you want us to."

"Not much to tell," she countered. "I was born in Independence. Went to school through eighth grade, and then my folks moved to Big Pine. Turned out to be a mistake. Dad fell in with even worse alcoholics than the ones in Independence, and he drank himself to death. I was just shy of sixteen then, and Mom ran off with a sweet-talking man who promised her the moon, but he was another drinker. I haven't seen her since."

"Anyone left but you and your brother?" Jed broke in.

She shook her head. "He got all fired up about Hunting shifters. This guy came through looking for recruits, and everyone with our blood has at least some magic." She sucked in a ragged breath. "By then, I'd moved out of Ma and Pa's place to get away from Abe—"

"That's your brother?" Les asked.

She nodded, silently begging him not to ask anything else about Abe. She couldn't stand to talk about her brother and everything he'd put her through. In a dark, secret corner of her mind, she felt ashamed she hadn't done more to get away from him. Sophie cleared her throat. "Anyway, Abe left with the man recruiting shifter Hunters. House was empty, so I moved back into it. Just a one room shack, really. No running water or anything, but it kept the rain and snow out."

"How long ago was that?" Jed asked.

"Almost eleven years. I just turned twenty-seven."

"It's a long time to plot revenge," Les said.

Heat swooshed from her chest over the top of her head. He'd caught her dead to rights. That was exactly why she hadn't left Big Pine—or the reservation. She was biding her time. Waiting until one of her visions brought her the news she'd been waiting for…

"What if it never happened?" Les inquired.

"What do you mean?" She turned to look at him and met the full force of a shrewd pair of amber eyes.

"Like Jed told you, reading thoughts is easy. What if you'd never seen your brother's death?"

"I don't know." She looked away, even more uncomfortable than she already was. "It had to happen. I prayed to every goddess out there. To all our spirit people—"

"There's more," Jed prodded.

Sophie ducked her head. Indeed there was, and shame threatened to swamp her. "I spent as much time as I could with our medicine man, when he wasn't too drunk to make sense. He taught me spells, incantations, weather working, and helped hone my visions."

The scent of the men's magic filled the car. Deeply soothing, it suggested she could tell them anything, anything at all. "Could I learn to do that?" she demanded.

"Do what?" Les asked, his eyes rounded into a picture of innocence.

"I feel your power. You're doing your utmost to pull information out of me, and it's working, although I'm not sure which things I'd say anyway, and which ones would've remained hidden."

"We don't know much about your magic," Les said. "Other than it's there. We feel it."

"And see it in an aura around you," Jed cut in. "We know Indian shamans who could nurture your magic, though, see how far it stretches."

"Really?" Excitement poured through her before she got hold of herself. She'd never let herself imagine life beyond the Big Pine Indian reservation.

"If you're dunning yourself for your brother's death, don't," Jed said flatly.

She slumped back against sweet-smelling leather seats. "I'm sure I have no idea—" she began.

"We believe in calling it like we see it," Les spoke over her. "You had every reason to hate your brother, and you worked magic to hasten his death."

"But it wasn't your magic that killed him," Jed said. "It was ours, coupled with his poor decision to align himself with Hunters."

Sophie clamped her jaws together until they ached. Even after everything Abe had done, she still harbored guilt for her midnight trips into the desert where she'd called on the spirit world to make him pay for hurting her, taking her innocence, and stripping her of her ability to feel anything for a man.

"No husbands, huh?" Les asked.

A bitter snort blew past her pursed lips. "Not even any boyfriends. I couldn't stand the thought of anyone else pawing at me."

"Eleven years is a long time," Jed repeated Les' earlier observation. "What'd you do besides plot Abe's death?"

"I read a lot. A bookmobile came through every month, and I'd check out books. I saved my Indian money and bought the Ford. When I had enough extra for gas, I'd drive to Bishop or Independence, mostly because there are libraries there." She stopped long enough to take a breath. "And I helped out in the school on the res—when we still had one. Lost our teacher this year, so the kids don't get to go to school unless they catch a ride into town."

"That's why no one will miss you for a while," Les said, sounding thoughtful.

She nodded. "They'll figure I went on one of my trips with the car. No one cared about where I went." Tears welled. "White men killed us when they forced us onto reservations. Our men are all drunks—most of them anyway, and the women aren't far behind. I worry what will become of my people."

"We have that in common," Jed said so softly, she wasn't certain she'd heard him.

"Guess you'd be worried about what happened today," she murmured.

"That's a hell of an understatement," Les said. Anger made his tone sharp. "Jed's been working with the other alphas, trying as hard as he can to find a way through to a peaceful solution, where we can live without being Hunted. Many of us are so sick of things, we want to kill every Hunter that walks the Earth, but Jed's reasoned with us—and with the other pack alphas."

"We were in the mountains to strategize peace," Jed said,

tightlipped. "Peace. And what did those fuckers do? Follow us. Threaten us. If we'd stayed in the cave and not fought back—"

"They'd have killed you," Sophie said, aware she'd interrupted him and shocked by how fierce her words sounded.

"Good you understand at least that part," Jed said.

"Oh, I understand plenty about being targeted by white man's laws." She stopped, swallowing hard. "You're white, but you understand what I mean. It's like they're looking for a scapegoat, someone to blame, someone they can label as bad. Once they've locked us up, they can shake hands all around and feel they've done their good deed for God and country." She slapped her palms together for emphasis.

"Which is exactly why shifters and Indians make such good allies," Les said. "Was your brother the only Indian mixed up with Hunters?"

She shook her head. "Of course not. They offered money, a ready escape from the res. Everyone who had the slightest hint of magic tried to get chosen. And the ones they turned down were bitterly disappointed." Sophie rolled her eyes. "One more excuse to hit the hooch."

Jed tapped the fuel gauge. "I'd better slow down. We filled up in Independence, but there's no gas between here and Mojave."

"Did you raise Alice and Megan?" Les asked.

Because she was watching him, Sophie saw the warm smile that curved the corners of Jed's mouth. "Yeah. They're on their way. Sophie might be stuck with us for a couple hours until they arrive, but Alice was so happy to hear from me, she dropped everything and was underway even before we were done talking. Megan too. I heard her chattering through our mind link."

Les broke into a broad grin. "Excellent. Means she's close enough for me to reach out to her telepathically."

Sophie's conscience smote her and she turned to Jed. "I'm sorry," she said softly.

"For what?" He glanced at her.

"Calling your mates sluts. I was out of line."

"I'm sorry too," he said. "For slapping you." Before she could respond, he hurried on. "I adore Alice. She's the center of my world, my universe. Bron, Terin, and I were alone forever. That we found a mate is nothing shy of a miracle. Les and Karl feel the same way about Megan."

Sophie leaned back in her seat, not sure what to say. She understood all too well about lonely and being alone. Her whole life had been like that, at least once her parents weren't there anymore. Was she a fool to trust the men sitting either side of her? Had they bewitched her in some way?

"Open your magic to me," Jed's voice sounded in her head, much like the medicine man's had done, when he wasn't too far gone to corral his power.

"I couldn't hear you before. Why can I now?"

"Because I dropped the shielding around my mind speech."

"I'm scared."

"Of course you are." His voice was deep and soothing, but she didn't sense his earlier compulsion spell. *"But if you open your magic, let it guide you, you'll discover you have nothing to fear."*

Sophie twisted her hands together until her knuckles turned white. The same choking sensation that had crippled her when her brother held her down and attacked her with his cock, closed her throat until breathing became a struggle.

"Hush. Ssht." Jed placed a gentle hand on her thigh.

Waves of calm washed through her. Because she was too conflicted to fight the sensation, her eyes fluttered shut, and she welcomed the healing sleep Jed sent her way.

CHAPTER 4

*L*es finished his telepathic conversation with Megan and turned to talk with Jed, but the wolf pack's alpha placed a finger over his lips. *"This way,"* Jed suggested. *"Sophie's sleeping."*

Les crinkled his brow, frowning. *"It's a spelled sleep."*

"That's right. She was exhausted and needed a break. Where are our women?"

"About two hours from Mojave."

Jed nodded. *"They made good time. It'll take us another hour to get there."*

"Did you make any progress?" Les glanced at Sophie.

Jed did too. The worried lines around her eyes had relaxed, and she looked younger, almost carefree. *"Some."* He ground his jaws together. *"That brother of hers did a real number on her when he raped her—repeatedly. She's never trusted anyone since. Not that I blame her, but it's going to take a while for her to warm to us—if she ever does."*

"Megan had a good idea," Les began.

Jed made come along motions with one hand.

36

"We need to find a family group for Sophie to join. Once she's mated, the bond will take care of any problems, and—"

"What makes you think she'll ever want any man anywhere near her again?" Jed broke in.

Les shrugged. *"The mate bond can be pretty damn compelling—if we found the right group of shifters. Ones who'd gentle her along."*

"I don't know if even that would work. You looked inside her mind. She hates sex and men."

"Well, Alice and Megan were chattering away about just that when I signed off. I filled them in on Sophie's background, and they didn't seem to think it would be an insurmountable problem since so many years have elapsed. Those two are nothing if not born matchmakers."

Jed snorted back laughter. He already knew that about Alice. She'd ferreted out half a dozen shifter mates since joining her life with his. Even talked about forming a group for the women since they often felt quite isolated. It wasn't as if they could have girlfriends or share much about their lives with anyone outside the pack.

"We'll take this one step at a time. Sophie aside, the backlash from what happened today is far more important. Our survival depends on it."

"Lot of unknowns, boss. Going to have to wait to see what comes down."

Jed knew that, and it grated on him. He relaxed what had turned into a death grip on the wheel. On his worst days, he wanted to take himself, Bron, Terin, and Alice far away. If they kept to themselves, they'd be fine, more than able to fly beneath the Hunters' radar. But he couldn't walk away from his obligation as alpha to his people. No. They'd stand together and either make it—or not.

"Want me to drive for a while?" Les asked softly.

Jed shook his head. "Nah. I'm fine."

Rolling desert studded with sagebrush flew past. The road wasn't paved, but it was still a decent surface. Sophie was an unexpected wrinkle, one they didn't need, but he couldn't turn her loose. Now that he knew more about her, he was pretty certain he couldn't bring himself to be the hand that ended her life, either. She'd suffered enough.

While she slept, he probed gently. Her magic was strong, as potent as any he'd found in a human. What did that mean? If her tribe's shaman hadn't been drunk all the time, would he have trained her to be their next medicine woman? Absent another Indian mage—despite his suggestion to her, he wanted to keep her presence in his home secret—could he entrain her power?

Jed frowned. He didn't know much about magic outside his own realm. But wolf shifter power was aligned with the earth. If her magic sprang from the same roots, maybe there'd be enough similarities for him to assist her. She'd already asked if she could learn the compulsion spell. And she'd flat out said she felt their magic eddying about her. Plus he could communicate telepathically with her.

Her magic was just one more item in a long list of unknowns.

He knew he was focused on Sophie to avoid thinking about the phalanx of undesirable consequences that could spring up from them murdering seventy-four Hunters. They hadn't left any traces, but still. If the law showed up with bloodhounds, they'd be able to track a scent trail. Possibly. Depending on if it was still raining hard in the Palisade Basin and maybe even snowing higher up on the glacier. As they'd driven south, the weather had cleared. Not warm, but not raining, either.

He checked behind him. The truck was still there, but Karl and Sophie's car were nowhere to be seen. He sent his mind voice spiraling out.

"I'm okay." Karl responded almost immediately. *"Car has an overheating problem, but I can core out the radiator and probably fix it for good—once we're home."*

"Sorry," Les broke in. *"He told me when I was talking with Megan. I figured you heard him, so I didn't say anything."*

"Where'd you stop?" Jed asked Karl.

"Not much in the way of landmarks, so it's more like when. I pulled onto a spur road about twenty minutes ago, but the car's cooled off and I'm ready to get underway again. Les said we're meeting the women in Mojave. Let me know which motel, and I'll get there when I get there."

"Good enough."

Jed glanced at a sign as it flashed past. They were few and far between on this stretch of road, but it said Mojave was another thirty miles. Not bad. They were closing on it. Next to him, Sophie stirred in her sleep and made a small, mewling noise. His heart went out to her. Maybe Megan and Alice were onto something. A shifter family group would prioritize her happiness, make certain she never wanted for anything.

The more he thought about it, the better he liked the idea. Sure she'd been roughly used, but she'd had years to move past it. And she was a woman now. Before she'd been nothing more than a frightened child.

Yes but why didn't she blow the whistle on him as she got older?

Jed chewed on his lip as he answered his own question. Being a victim grew into a habit where the person just went along with the status quo because it was easier than making waves.

His eyes widened and he pounded a fist on the wheel, making the car swerve unexpectedly.

"What?" Les' startled voice blasted into his mind, and Jed felt the other shifter gather power.

"Stand down," he said. *"We're not under attack. I just figured something important out."*

SOPHIE WOKE to find the car had stopped next to a small creek, and she was alone in the cab. She'd never been south of Independence before, so had no idea where they were. Before she could ask or look around for the men, who had to be close, Jed tugged one of the car doors open.

"Come on outside. I felt the shift in your energy and knew you were awake."

Rotating her shoulder blades to get some feeling back into them, she was pleased to discover her jacket wasn't nearly as soaked as it had been. She slid out of the car and scanned the desert around them. Greenery hugged the water, but sand, rocks, and sagebrush peppered the land everywhere else.

Bron, Terin, and Les got up from where they'd been seated next to the creek. Les walked over to her and held out his hand. Raw fish fillets lay across his palm. "Fishing's good here," he said. "Would you like some trout?"

"Raw?" She closed her teeth over her lower lip. "I am hungry, but..."

"Try it," he suggested. "It's sweet when it's fresh like this."

She filched a sliver of the translucent flesh and popped it into her mouth, chewing slowly. Flavor exploded in her mouth, and she reached for a second piece.

Les smiled. "I had a feeling you'd like it. Go ahead, sister. Take all of what's in my hand. We caught several."

"Where are we?" she asked around mouthfuls of the succulent fish. "And what happened to Karl? Did my car strand him somewhere?"

The sound of a familiar engine answered her last two questions, and Karl pulled to a stop next to the car and truck. He exited her car and stretched.

"I know exactly how you feel," she called. "That spring under your butt gets old after a few miles."

"I've driven worse."

Les handed him a whole fish, and Karl dragged a knife from a pocket and proceeded to gut and skin it.

"To answer your other question—" Jed moved closer "—we're about five miles north of Mojave. I wanted to wait for Karl and our mates out here rather than in the middle of town."

"No kidding." Terin rolled his eyes. "Better if we check into a motel as couples than a big group of men with one woman. Looks bad."

"There're still five of you and three women," Sophie pointed out. She'd inhaled the fish and made her way to the creek where she squatted, cupped water into her hands, and drank.

"True enough," Terin replied. "Jed and Alice will get a room. Either Les or Karl and Megan will get another. Bron or I will get a room with you."

Old familiar terror, laced with a healthy dollop of anger, raced through her, and Sophie backed away. She reached for the knife she always kept strapped close in a thigh sheath and brandished it. "I don't think so," she said through clenched teeth.

"Bad choice of words," Jed cut in smoothly. "Terin was just telling you how we'd split up the rooms, not who'd be sleeping in them." He eyed her knife, his blue eyes dancing with something she couldn't decipher. "Sloppy of us not to frisk you."

Sophie glared at him through slitted eyes. All the concerns that had pounded her earlier returned in force. Was trusting Jed—or any of them—a huge mistake? She had the knife in hand, but now that they knew about it, they'd make her give it to them. Before she could think about her choice, she twisted the blade until it lay against the side of her neck.

"Don't come any closer, any of you," she warned. "I'd rather die than have another man touch me against my will."

"I get that." Jed stood still. So did the others. When he spoke again, his voice was low, soothing, but devoid of magic. Maybe he understood how close she was to plunging the knife into the big vessels at the side of her neck and being done with everything. Abe was dead. Revenge was the only thing she'd lived for, and now the deed was done. No matter whose magic had killed him, her brother was gone. He'd never hurt anyone again.

"The best revenge is living well," Karl said.

She twisted her face into a grimace. "Fucker! You were in my head." Her voice rose to a scream. "All of you. You're probably all inside my head."

"Yes. Because we care about you." Jed still didn't make any moves in her direction. "I didn't speak up for you in front of the other clan leaders only to have you kill yourself. Pull your head out of your ass and learn how to respect your own life."

The words shocked her. And made her angry. "How dare you," she hissed, moving toward him. "You have no idea what it was like to live my life. To hear Abe stumble into the house and head right for me."

"And you have no idea," he countered, "what it's like to be hunted. To live a double life because if you didn't, you'd be gunned down or slapped in a prison cell."

"The res is a whole lot like a prison cell." She shrugged awkwardly, not letting go of the knife.

"It's not the same." Bron skewered her with his dark gaze. "You can leave anytime. You might be scared or trapped into staying because you don't have to pay rent for your house, but you're still free. The white man may have stripped you of your pride, but he stopped hunting you in the early nineteen hundreds."

"1924," she shot back. "Last Apache war ended twelve years ago."

"Fine." He tossed his hand in front of him. "I stand corrected on dates, but I agree with Jed. You'd get a whole lot farther if you stopped feeling sorry for yourself."

"And expecting the worst out of every male who crosses your path," Terin added.

"We're not all rapists," Karl countered. "In truth, the vast majority of us aren't."

The knife trembled where she held it against her throat because her hand shook so badly. No one had ever talked to her like that before. No one had ever said a word about Abe, good, bad, or indifferent. As if by holding silence, they didn't have to address her outrage.

She lowered her arm, and the knife clattered to the dirt at her feet. Tears sat perilously close to the surface, but she swallowed them back. "Aren't you going to grab my knife?" she demanded.

"I'd rather you handed it over," Jed said, "but if you want to tuck it back into your thigh sheath, I'm good with that."

She fell back a pace. "Why would you let me keep something I could hurt you with?"

"Oh, sweetie." Terin shook his head. "If you'd been wired that way, you'd have tried something in the car."

Jed moved closer, but still maintained some distance between them. "I'm not adverse to you being able to defend yourself—against bad guys. That's not us."

A tear spilled over. She ignored it and reached for her knife, tucking it beneath her long, woolen skirt.

The roar of another car engine attracted her attention. They weren't that far off the road, but traffic was very thin. Jed's head snapped up, and a warm smile wreathed his face, making his blue eyes light from within. He pushed his red gold hair away from his face and ran to where a shiny, new Ford Cabriolet was heading right for them.

The car skidded to a halt in a rain of gravel, and the two front doors flew open. Tall women piled out. As tall as she was. The driver had waist-length coal black hair and dancing green eyes. The other woman was blonde with sky-blue eyes. All the men hurried over to them. Bron, Jed, and Terin surrounded the dark-haired woman and Les and Karl drew the blonde into a warm embrace.

The men rained kisses and murmured endearments on their mates. The moment grew so intimate, Sophie looked away, feeling she was trespassing on something sacred. What came through loud and clear was the love these men and women held for one another. It underscored her loneliness. No one had ever loved her like that. She'd never come first with anyone, not even her parents. Maybe it was her imagination that anyone back in Big

Pine would even notice she'd left. After all, one less mouth meant more food to go around.

What? Am I going to sink into a pity party? Poor Sophie and all that rot?

Get over it.

She made her way back to the creek. Water splashed merrily over stones, singing joyfully. All the running water in this area probably dried up come midsummer, but it was December. Short days and winter in the offing. A flash of silver caught her eye as two fat trout swam past.

A small voice deep inside urged her to run. This was her chance. The men were busy greeting their mates. There'd never be a better time. She glanced behind her. Everyone was still hugging and kissing. They'd never notice if she slunk off.

The hell they wouldn't.

They'd find me, and it wouldn't be pretty.

Worse, she was of two minds about running. Part of her was beginning to trust Jed and the others, believed they were good men—despite being shifters. When it got right down to it, she didn't know very much about men with dual natures beyond the legends. What Les said was right. Once upon a time, many Indians had been shifters, and maybe some still were, just not in her tribe. In a misguided attempt to mollify the white man, the Paiutes had jumped on the anti-shifter bandwagon. Easy enough, since they hadn't had to hang any of their own out to dry.

Footsteps behind her made Sophie jump to her feet and turn to face whoever was coming. The women converged on her, sweeping her into heartfelt embraces.

"I'm Alice Carey," the brunette announced, followed by, "Oopsie. Guess my last name is actually Starnes now. Not used to it quite yet."

"And I'm Megan Galen." The blonde grinned, showing very straight teeth. "The fellows and I aren't legally married—yet. We haven't found the time, so I don't have Alice's last name problems."

Feeling suddenly shy, Sophie looked away from the frank appraisal in the other women's gazes. "Sophie," she said.

"What's your last name, honey?" Alice asked.

"Which one?" Sophie quirked a brow.

"How about all of them?" Megan laughed, warm and rich as fresh-churned butter.

Sophie felt her cheeks heat. "My white man's name is Fuller. My Indian name is Laughing Wolf."

"Aha!" Alice's green eyes glittered mischievously. "You'll fit right in."

"You will indeed," Megan seconded. "No wonder the boys brought you along."

"They don't know," Sophie said.

"We do now." Jed drew close and draped a familiar arm around his mate.

Alice lifted her face and he brushed his lips across hers before turning back to Sophie. "Anyway, hon, here's the plan. We're headed into town with all the cars. The guys will sort out how the rooms in the motel end up getting registered, but Megan and I will tag team staying with you tonight. Sound okay?"

"Tag team?" Sophie frowned, not quite understanding.

"What she means—" Megan bent close "—is Alice will spent some time loving her mates while I'm with you, and then we'll trade."

Sophie stiffened. "So long as none of this trading involves me, I'm good with it."

"Not to worry." Alice's expression turned serious. "If you laid so much as a fingernail on my men, I'd flay you alive."

"Not that I want Les or Karl in, um, that way—" Sophie focused on Megan "—but do you feel the same?"

"You bet, sweetie." Megan had stopped smiling too. "One of the things Alice and I want to make sure happens tonight while we're swinging-door roommates is talking with you about shifter mate bonds."

"Oh, it's really not necessary—" Sophie began.

Alice spoke over her. "Yeah, it is. You're going to be part of us from now on, and you have to understand how things work." She paused a beat. "I wish I'd had someone to explain the ropes to me, but I had to figure things out on my own. Made a bunch of mistakes and almost got myself and Jed killed because of my stupidity."

"Sounds like an interesting story," Sophie murmured.

"It is. Maybe that's what we'll start with later tonight."

"What do all of you want to do about dinner?" Jed asked.

"Oh, let's go out," Alice slipped an arm through her mate's.

"If the town is jumping, we'll do just that." He gifted her with one of his brilliant smiles.

"And if it's not?" she asked.

"We'll stop at the local market and figure out what we can cook," Bron replied. "God, but it's good to see you, sweetheart."

"You too." Alice's green eyes softened. "When days went by with no word, Megan and I were plenty worried."

Jed glanced at his watch. "I don't want anyone to overhear any of this, so the boys and I will fill you in before we drive into Mojave."

"Excellent!" Megan clapped her hands together and leaned into her mates, who stood right behind her.

"You won't be doing much hand clapping once you hear what happened," Sophie muttered and could've kicked herself. "Sorry." She angled her head Jed's way. "Your people. Your story."

CHAPTER 5

Sophie plumped up two pillows behind her back and leaned on the wall her bed butted against. They hadn't made it into Mojave until well after dark. Predictably, Alice and Megan had been frantic once they heard the men's tale. They'd asked a million questions—and shed more than a few tears. Despite the late hour, a roadside grill had been crowded with cars, and they'd stopped for dinner before locating the motor hotel where they'd secured four rooms, enough to avoid suspicion from the desk clerk.

After a whispered consultation with Megan, Alice had drawn first watch, even though the women weren't calling it that. She stretched her long-legged frame across the other bed and laid on her stomach with her head propped on a fisted hand.

"Jed told me that you're no stranger to magic." Alice kept her voice low. "I'm going to draw a small power circle to make certain our words remain within it."

Sophie nodded. "I understand things like that." She sensed the other woman's enchantment build around her. It had the same feel as the men's, mildly electric and tasting of forests and wild things. "Did your mates teach you magic?"

"Of course, and I absorbed everything I have through the shifter mate bond." Alice narrowed her eyes and focused on Sophie. "I'd originally planned to tell you a bunch of stuff, but maybe it would work better if you asked me questions. That way, you'll get what you need, and not have to wade through things that might not be important to you."

"You seem happy." Sophie rolled her eyes. "It's not exactly a question, but you're not anything like I thought you'd be."

"What?" Alice furled her dark brows. "Too normal?"

"Are you happy with Jed and Bron and Terin?" Sophie persisted, sidestepping Alice's query. No way would she tell her that she'd assumed all shifter mates were over-sexed sluts. "Tell me how that works. I don't understand why the men aren't snarling and fighting over you."

"Because they love each other as well as me."

"Does that mean what I think it does?" Sophie wrapped her arms around herself prepared for almost anything.

"Probably not. The men aren't sexual with each other. Oh they tease about sex, but they're firmly into women, not each other." Alice paused to take a breath. "When I said they loved each other, I meant that they're a family. They were family hundreds of years before I came into their life. Think of them as a band of brothers."

Sophie was still stuck on the previous sentence. "Hundreds of years?" she repeated, fighting disbelief.

"Oh yeah. Shifters are long lived. I will be too since they shared their magic with me, but I won't live as long as they do."

"Have you ever been sorry you linked your life to theirs?"

"Not for so much as a second—once I came to my senses and realized what a gift they'd offered me."

"How'd you meet them?"

"Now there's a story," Alice said. "Probably the important part was I saw shifters the same way you do before Jed crossed my path. I believed they were wicked, evil, that they ate boiled babies for breakfast. That kind of thing."

She jackknifed her body into a sitting position and walked to Sophie's bed where she perched on the edge. "When I first met Jed, I was a virgin. Couldn't for the life of me figure out why I wanted him so much I couldn't think of anything except getting into bed with him. It was the mate bond at work, and he explained it to me the morning after we met, but he failed to mention Bron or Terin."

Alice shook her head and then went on, "To Jed's credit, he meant to, but they showed up before he had a chance. I've always had a temper, and I blew a fuse. Accused him of signing me up for plural marriage hell and other equally shitty things. Because I was furious, I ran off halfcocked into the forest, and a mountain lion attacked me. Jed took his wolf form and fought the cat. Bron and Terin helped. At the end of things, my shoulder was torn to shreds, and Jed almost died.

"Bron is one of the most talented healers in the clans. He saved his alpha, and Terin patched me up. By the time we were all more or less whole again, I'd come to my senses and the mate bond was spinning its magic."

"Say more about that." Sophie leaned forward.

"Which part?"

"The shifter mate bond." Sophie lowered her voice. "I've heard rumors for years that it turned decent women into harlots and that shifters forced their women into sick, twisted group sex with whole roomfuls of men. I'm guessing none of that's true."

"Not sure about the harlot part, but I was so taken with Jed, I was afraid I'd turned nympho." Alice twisted her mouth into a wry smile. When she laughed, it broke the tension simmering in Sophie's gut. "All I can tell you is that lovemaking with my mates is the most amazing, life-shattering experience imaginable. I dream about them when I'm not with them, and I look forward to everything we do together."

"Do the men ever, um, include others?" Sophie felt herself blushing at the graphic nature of her question.

"Of course not. They love me. They'd kill any other man who laid a hand on me that way."

"So it's kind of like having three husbands, like the Mormons have multiple wives?"

"Well, I've never been a Mormon, but I suspect I have far more freedom than their women. I only recently quit working, and it was my decision, not the men's."

Sophie bit her lower lip, thinking. "You have three mates. Megan has two. What determines that? Are there ever more than three or just one?"

"Shifters form family groups, made up of two or three of them. I suppose it might end up being just one if the others were killed."

"I got the impression all of you live together..." Sophie's cheeks grew even warmer, and the second part of her question died unspoken. Frank discussions about sex had never been part of her life.

"We do," Alice said matter-of-factly. "Jed and them have an enormous house in the Hollywood Hills. We were visiting Les and Karl, and the men ran into a spot of trouble. They needed to get out of Canada and were newly mated to Megan, so we invited them to come home with us. That was a few weeks ago, and it's worked out so well, they're still there. And no—" Alice slitted her eyes at Sophie "—we don't get into group sex with them, and it isn't because we haven't had the opportunity. It's not how things work."

"This mate bond, it's specific to each family group?"

Alice nodded. "You'd make a perfect shifter mate."

The words came with no warning, and a bomb going off next to Sophie wouldn't have startled her more. "Me?" The word came out as a squeak. "Oh hell, no. I hate men. I hate sex. I—" Her tongue twisted into a knot, and no more words came.

"Oh, honey." Alice patted her leg. "Jed told me what that monster brother of yours did to you. Are you going to give him what he wanted after all?"

"I have no idea what you mean," Sophie said stiffly. "He's dead."

Something feral and fraught with wisdom flared deep in Alice's green eyes. "Good thing he got what he deserved—finally. But he set out to ruin your life. Why are you letting him?"

"I— I'm not," Sophie sputtered.

"A good man—or men—could make you very happy. Don't discard the idea out of hand." Alice smiled like a Madonna. "Just because your brother was an asshole doesn't mean all men are."

Sophie shrugged uncomfortably. "Well, all this is conjecture, right? It's not as if there's a shifter pack banging down the door looking for a mate."

"It's a shifter family group," Alice corrected with a smile. "As for the other, I have a few in mind that you might blend with really well. Turns out I have a knack for that kind of thing."

"Matchmaking?" Sophie's eyes widened, and a combination of fear and something else she didn't have a name for pushed shivers down her spine.

"Another aspect to consider," Alice plowed on, seemingly oblivious to Sophie's inner turmoil, "is that your magic would grow by leaps and bounds after an infusion of shifter power. Your Indian talents would blend nicely with shifter abilities. I met a medicine woman in Canada who'd married into a shifter family group. She was stronger than Jed in some ways and could spin the most incredible spells. Why, she created an illusion that let Megan escape from jail."

"Why do I get the sense there's another story there?" Sophie grinned in spite of her reservations.

"Oh there is, but I'll let Megan tell it to you. Meantime, think about what I've said. At least hold an open mind."

"I will."

"Good." Alice jerked her chin downward and scrunched her face into a mass of concerned lines. "This is somewhat self-serving of me, but if we can get you mated, it'll be one less headache for the guys. What happened in the mountains is a powder keg, and it could blow with us on top of it. We might have to go on the run, disappear somewhere. The men haven't said anything directly, but between Meg and me, we do a fair job reading their minds."

"But how will you live?" Concern for her new friends sluiced through Sophie.

"There's plenty of money. It's one of the side benefits of shifters living so long. I think Jed still has a manor house or two in either Europe or northern England, and I know Les and Karl have castles in Germany."

"Things aren't any better for shifters over there," Sophie muttered. "Not from what I read in the newspapers."

"Grist for the mill." Alice focused her direct gaze on Sophie. "Even knowing what I do, I'd chose Jed again given a choice. He's everything to me. Him and Bron and Terin."

"Thanks for being so honest. It's been a long time since I've had much of anyone to talk with."

"You're welcome. I have a feeling you'd do the same for me."

A muted knock sounded on the door just before Megan walked in looking flushed and disheveled. "How's the girl gab fest coming along?" she inquired archly.

"Really well," Alice replied. She got to her feet and bent to kiss the top of Sophie's head. "Welcome to our pack, sister."

"But I don't, I mean, I haven't—"

"Yes, but you will. Use that gift of farseeing to check out your own future," Alice said firmly before turning and walking out the door Megan hadn't quite latched shut.

JED, Bron, and Terin stood at the edge of the motor hotel's large parking lot. They were using the time Alice spent with Sophie to dissect what had happened in the Palisade Basin.

"You know how I've argued against striking back hard against our enemies?" Jed asked.

"Of course," Bron replied. "You've held us back many a time when we would've taken a far more aggressive stance."

"We got lucky with that Hunter friend of Alice's," Terin said.

"Not so much, I scrambled his brain enough, his one-way ticket to the asylum didn't surprise me," Bron muttered.

"Ha!" Jed elbowed him. "Finally admitting it, huh?"

"Yes, but what of it?"

"I had an epiphany when we were driving down here." Jed moved to where he could look at both his lieutenants.

"We're waiting," Terin said, but the usual bantering tone had left his voice.

Jed nodded. "I was thinking about Sophie and why she didn't fight back against her brother once she got old enough."

"What'd you come up with?" Bron asked. "Because I wondered the same thing."

"Being a victim grows into a habit where the person rides out the status quo because it's easier than making waves." Jed growled not unlike his wolf would have. "It didn't take a crystal ball for me to understand it's the same thing I've done. I've been so invested in keeping a low profile, staying off people's radar screens, that I cemented our victim status."

"It wasn't as bad as all that—" Terin began.

"Oh yeah, it was." Jed jabbed the air with his fist. "If we'd stood up for ourselves at the front end of this whole fuck fest, we'd have seen a few more casualties, but I bet we wouldn't be at the shit end of the stick where we are now."

"Kind of like the Native Americans and the whole reservation deal, huh?" Bron said thoughtfully. "They let the white man kick them from here to there to crappy land no one else wanted."

"Exactly."

"What are you thinking of doing?" Terin asked.

"The clan alphas will show up six days from now. I want to

draw up a list of demands we can present to the powers that be here in the United States. If they ignore us—or worse, imprison whoever went to Washington—it'll mean all-out war."

"You've always said we'd lose," Bron spoke slowly.

"Yeah." Jed flashed a bitter smile at his lieutenant. "And we may, but what we've been doing isn't really living. We're hiding, scuttling at the edges of the shadows and hoping against hope today isn't the day someone puts two and two together and figures out what we are." He stopped to suck in a breath. "And they will, you know. Someday, the gig will be up, and then where will we be?"

Terin nodded solemnly. "I'm behind you, no matter what."

"So am I," Bron chimed in, "but then, you knew that."

"There you are." Alice's voice drifted from across the parking lot. "What are you all doing out here?"

"Enjoying the moon, sweetheart." Jed circled their mate with an arm once she stepped close.

"It is lovely." She turned her face to gaze at it, looking beautiful and vulnerable.

Not that there'd been a shred of doubt, but that moment solidified Jed's resolve to make certain his mate was safe. Now and always. If it came to war, he'd put her on a ship for Europe. She'd fight leaving him, but he'd insist…

"Jed?"

"Yes, love."

"You felt pretty far away there for a moment."

"How about if we go inside?" Terin suggested. "You can tell us what progress you made with Sophie."

"I like inside," Bron said, lowering his voice. "It's on the way to our room."

Jed punched him playfully. "We all like that part. Shall we?"

He listened to the crunch of boot soles as they navigated the huge parking lot to the motor hotel's front door and hoped to hell his *take a stand* strategy wouldn't blow up in his face. He'd kick it around with Keir and Jon and Blake, but if the other alphas agreed, it'd be all systems full steam ahead.

Deep inside, relief coursed through him. He'd been a long time coming to this point, and if they hadn't stumbled across Sophie, the perspective he needed to guide his people forward might've continued to elude him.

He'd make a point of thanking her come morning.

CHAPTER 6

Sophie curled on her side with a book. It was late, past midnight, and she was working at reading herself to sleep. A few days had passed since the group welcomed her into their home. Enough time that she was coming to care about them. Alice and Megan had been nothing but kind, and the men treated her with respect as well. She might be their prisoner, but it didn't feel that way. An unexpected side benefit was an entire room chock full of books covering everything from fiction to history. In many ways it was better stocked than the small libraries in Bishop and Independence, where she'd lost herself in different worlds.

When she dissected her feelings, she was shocked to realize she didn't want to leave. Even if Jed opened the front door and told her that he trusted she'd keep her mouth shut, it would've been hard to wave goodbye and walk through it. She was happier in this sprawling Hollywood Hills mansion than she'd been in her life—probably ever.

Not feeling particularly sleepy, and not wanting to read, either, she got to her feet and walked to the glass door that opened onto a small patio. Her room was on the third floor, so no one worried she'd launch an escape, but they probably knew she wasn't a flight risk any longer. Pulling the door open, she walked outside. Fragrant night smells greeted her, and she inhaled hungrily.

The men's magic nurtured an extensive array of greenery—from shrubs surrounding the basement swimming pool, to exotic flowers and trees lining the estate's grounds. Other scents tickled her nostrils too. Lovemaking. The muted sound of people enjoying one another reached her, and she felt suddenly lonely.

Alice's question about why she'd allowed Abe to cut her off from the possibility of sharing her life with a man rose to taunt her, as did the woman's intimation she'd make a perfect shifter mate.

In the time since she'd arrived, Alice and Megan had made a point of introducing her to many wolf shifters, but she hadn't felt anything in particular. Maybe that part of her truly was broken. According to the woman, when the mate bond struck, it was worse than a lightning bolt, impossible to ignore. Nothing even close had happened with any of the men who'd shared their table. Or who'd dropped in, hoping she might be their chosen one.

Not that they weren't attractive, well-spoken, and probably just as kind and caring as Jed and the rest of them, but nothing had sparked. She'd noticed Alice and Megan exchanging pointed glances and figured the women could talk without words—just like their men. She'd wanted to know what passed between them, but been too shy to ask, and it felt rude to try to listen in. Were they feeling sorry for her? Or worse, chalking her up as a hopeless case?

Why not? I gave up on myself a long time ago.

Truth in her thoughts drew her up short. Maybe it was time to rethink things. If she didn't, she'd be nothing but a victim for the rest of her days. Abe may be dead, but Alice hit the nail on its head when she pointed out that he was still dogging her every thought, action, and footstep.

Crap!

She pinched the bridge of her nose between her thumb and

forefinger. What would happen next? The men had some kind of major meeting scheduled for tomorrow or the next day. It had the feel of her people before they took a stand. Except every time that happened, the Paiutes lost.

Not the same, she told herself. Alcohol had all but ruined her tribe. They got liquored up and talked big, even did some posturing, but they backed down quick enough too. She had a feeling if the shifter clans drew a line in the sand, they'd defend it to the death.

Breath burned the back of her throat, and she swallowed back tears. If something happened to those she was coming to see as her adoptive family, the pain would tear her into shreds of misery. Sophie straightened her spine. She'd do everything in her power to help Jed and the other shifters and their mates. Maybe her magic, weak as it was, might be something they could use. Snapshots of the future were always helpful. Resolved to at least offer, she went back inside and crawled into bed, turning out her bedside light.

Sighs and soft words of love drifted to her when she opened her magic. At first, she pushed them away, but then she allowed the energy of the shifters' lovemaking to fill her with longing. Sophie ran her hands over her body, tentatively at first. She'd always avoided any touches not specifically associated with keeping herself clean, so she pulled her fingers away from her flesh several times before she allowed them to remain.

The skin in the hollow of her collarbones was soft and sensitive. Her rounded breasts felt good as she kneaded them, rubbing their nipples into peaks that made her breath catch in her throat. Keeping a hand on one breast, she ran the other down her ribcage, across her flat stomach, and traced the lines of her hipbones.

When her fingers brushed the edges of the soft curls surrounding her sex, she stopped. What she was doing felt perverse, wrong, even though she longed to stroke lower, to discover if her body was capable of response in a totally non-threatening situation.

"If I can't get past touching myself," she murmured, "how the hell will I ever let anyone else get near me, without hiding behind a wall and pretending nothing is happening. Just like I did all those hundreds of times with Abe?"

She bit down on her lower lip hard enough to hurt and pushed exploratory fingers downward. They tangled in the hair at the entrance to her sex before she smoothed it out of the way and stroked the slick skin beneath. A jolt of pleasure shot through her. It was such a surprise, she drew her hand up and away from whatever had felt so good.

Breathing shallowly, she opened her magic wider and drew in the sensual rhythm filling the house. Everyone was making love. She sensed Jed, Bron, Terin, and Alice, limbs entwined, bringing everyone to peaks of delight. From the opposite end of the house, the energy flowing from Les, Karl, and Megan felt different, but just as intense.

Sophie dropped her hand over her sex again, cupping herself. The heat from her hand made her hips twitch in anticipation. She knew about sexual climax. Of course she did. God knew, Abe had enough of them—at her expense.

"No!" She shook her head—and left her hands where they were. "No more about my perverted brother. I let him rule my life for far too long."

Resolute, she banished him from her thoughts and concentrated on teasing the nipple she still held. She pressed against the hand over her woman's parts. When it didn't seem like quite enough, she stroked herself with a tentative finger, finding the place that created such intensity.

Once there, she teased, tweaked, stroked, and rubbed. Her heartrate quickened, and her breath was loud against the silence of her room. Her nipple grew harder, and the nub between her legs that captured her attention swelled too. Unfamiliar feelings swirled deep in her belly, and heat cascaded over her in waves. Against her closed lids, she imagined a mythical male body touching her, lying next to her, pressing his hard-muscled form close as he slashed his lips over hers.

Dream man was blond with very blue eyes. He whispered how stunning she was, how he could barely wait to make her his. The rhythm of her rubbing intensified, and her hips bucked against her hand. Sensation spilled through her so hot, sweet, and intense she cried out. And hoped to hell no one heard.

She worked her slick folds until her body quieted. The same spark she'd stoked into a climax still burned, a glowing ember rather than a raging fire, but she was pretty sure she could make the same cascade of scorching heat happen again.

Pushing herself to a sit, she walked across the room and looked out onto a moonlit night. The wonder of what her body was capable of buffeted her. If she'd known, maybe she would have put Abe behind her long since.

Maybe not.

Some things require long healing, and that was one of them.

When she cast her magic wide, the others were still deeply involved. Good. It meant they wouldn't have been paying one whit of attention to her. Deeply pleased her sexuality wasn't terminally damaged, as she'd feared it might be, she padded back to bed. When she closed her eyes this time, sleep was quick to answer her call.

BLAKE DROVE through the star-studded night. One of his lieutenants sat next to him, the other sprawled across the backseat snoring softly. They'd be a day early arriving at Jed's but better early than late. Besides, it would give him an opportunity to get down and dirty with Jed. The more he'd thought about the woman Jed spared, the less he liked it. Better to take care of business once and for all. Much as he respected Jed, the wolf clan's alpha was too soft-hearted for his own good.

"Wish I'd have been there," Gideon muttered from the passenger seat. "Next time you decide we're better off at home guarding our people, I'll challenge you over it."

Blake swallowed a snort. "You're just annoyed because you missed a good fight."

"Yeah. That too." Gideon raked his hands through coal black hair. Like all coyote shifters, he was tall and lanky. He focused his ink-dark gaze on Blake and gathered the ends of his hair into a sloppy braid.

"I suppose you and Mac had a heyday discussing what a shit I was for leaving you home?" Blake cast a sidelong glance at his lieutenant.

"Wouldn't go that far." Mac's sleepy voice sounded from the backseat. "We did talk about it, though. Especially once you were close enough for telepathy and told us what happened."

"Exactly." Blake let the one word hang in the air.

Mac rustled around and came to a sitting position. "Maybe I'm still half asleep, boss, but what did you mean by that?"

Breath whistled past Blake's teeth. "I had no idea what would happen at the last clan gathering. Nowhere in my wildest imaginings did I expect Hunters to attack us. Once they did, it was even more important to have the two of you in position to protect our people and launch countermeasures—if it became necessary."

"But you expected it to just be a meeting," Gideon protested.

"True," Blake replied, "but I believe in being prepared. We finally have enough mated family groups that there are children. What would've become of them if we'd all been in the Sierras?"

"But nothing happened," Mac muttered. "Nothing at all. So little, here we are with you heading for Los Angeles."

"L.A. may not be much closer to Vegas than where I was before," Blake countered, "but the roads are much faster. Plus, I prepared everyone. We have a fallback position, a place to meet in case the authorities get energetic about hunting us down."

"You mean more energetic," Mac groused. "Bastards." His flame red hair caught the reflection of a passing pair of headlights.

"Not to change the subject," Gideon cut in, "but where are we staying tonight?"

Blake glanced at his watch and then at the surrounding countryside. They were about an hour outside the city, and it would take another thirty minutes once they got there to wend their way up to Jed's place. "I figured we'd bunk with Jed. Why?"

"It's the middle of the night," Gideon said. "Hate to wake them."

"They're wolves. Bet they stay up late—just like us. You have something in mind, Gid. What?"

"You know me too well, boss."

"Shame on me if I didn't by now," Blake retorted.

"Aw Jesus, you two," Mac broke in. "Cut the crap. Gid, what're you thinking? And before you speak up, there's nothing but desert around us. We could pull off on a side road, shift, and play for an hour or two. That way, it would at least be dawn by the time we show up at Jed's place."

"Took the words right out of my mouth, bro," Gideon flashed a grin over one shoulder.

"That what you boys want to do?" Blake asked. The idea held a certain appeal. Coyotes were natural born desert creatures. There'd be local animals to gather news from too.

"Yeah. Sounds great," Mac said.

Blake hunted for a sandy road that led away from the highway. Once he found a promising candidate, he followed it until the roar of the highway muted to almost nothing, and drew the car to a stop. He pushed his door open and took a deep breath, filling his lungs with the dry desert air. It was cold, but not uncomfortably so, and the night smelled of sagebrush and small rodents scurrying as fast and as far as they could. Humans might not know what his kind were, but everybody in the animal kingdom knew they were different.

Mac and Gideon pulled off clothing, stacking it in the Chrysler Airstream convertible. A creamy white color, it gleamed in moonlight flirting with them through the clouds.

"Gonna undress, boss?" Mac's hazel eyes gleamed with anticipation. Clearly, he couldn't wait to find his coyote form.

One of the reasons both he and Gideon were so put out about missing the fight in the Palisades was because everyone had fought in shifted form, a rarity these days. Rather than answering, Blake kicked off his loafers and stripped off his socks, dropping both in the driver's foot well. His dark green wool trousers came next, followed by his shorts. Last of all, he slid a black cashmere sweater off his shoulders and unbuttoned his ivory silk shirt.

The air shimmered, flashing brightly as Mac and Gideon transitioned into coyotes. In line with their human coloration, Mac's pelt was red-brown, while Gideon's gleamed dusky black. The pair flashed their tails his way and took off at a dead run, howling and yipping their glee.

Blake grinned. He'd give damn near anything for a world where his kind could shift at will, but that world hadn't existed for hundreds of years. He plucked the keys from the ignition and tucked them beneath a front tire before slamming all the doors and calling for his own animal. His molecules had barely finished transforming when he raced after his lieutenants.

The sand beneath his paws felt amazingly good, and he dug his claws in for good measure. The rodents he'd smelled in his human form blasted his sensitive coyote senses, and saliva dripped from his jaws. A field mouse, who'd apparently missed the memo that it was time to flee, skittered into view. Blake lunged, breaking its neck, and bit into sweet flesh. Hot blood flooded his mouth and he chewed, crunching through fragile bones.

By the time he caught up with Mac and Gideon, they sat on their haunches in a circle with half a dozen local coyotes. He joined them, howling like mad things until they broke and ran, chasing one another and hunting game until their breath steamed in the chill night air. Many mice, two voles, and a badger later, they trotted back toward where they'd left the car.

The local crew, who'd helped subdue the badger, headed for their dens. They fully understood Blake, Mac, and Gideon were different, and they didn't ask questions. Their kind never dug too deep into something they'd never understand. Coyotes weren't big on wasting energy if they could help it.

Blake glanced at the moon where it hung low on the horizon. The eastern sky was lightening a little, which meant dawn was close but not upon them yet. All the better. Shifting was far safer under nighttime's protective cloak. Guilt stabbed him. Not shifting at all—particularly in light of the firestorm sure to descend on them soon—was by far the safest path, but he'd never been a coward.

Stupid, yes, but not shy on courage. What a shitty combination.

He chortled inwardly and was still laughing once he was human again.

"What's so funny?" Gideon slid well-worn leather trousers up his legs.

"Yeah," Mac broke in. "We'd like a good laugh too."

"Foolhardy of us to shift—especially right now."

"Okay, but how's that funny?" Mac looked inside the car. "Where'd you hide the keys? I can drive for a while."

"Behind the left front tire. It was only humorous in context," Blake said. "Not worth worrying about."

They piled back inside the car with Mac behind the wheel. Blake was still grinning. Mac loved driving the plush Chrysler. They all did. The powerful engine was wonderfully responsive.

"What would you think about us stopping at a diner for breakfast?" Gideon asked from the backseat.

"Not much," Blake replied. "I really do want to chew the fat with Jed. It's why I set out a day early. So we'd have time before the other two alphas show up."

"You want to make certain the woman dies, right?" Mac glanced at his alpha before returning his attention to the road. They'd reached the highway and were headed west again.

"That and I want to impress upon Jed that we have to strike hard and fast. This hiding out and laying low strategy will be our undoing. Battle mode may well end up a different downfall, but at least we'll die with swords in our hands and not cowering in the back of our dens."

"Love the analogy, boss, but we haven't fought with swords for a long time." Gideon chuckled.

"Yeah, yeah, and we don't live in dens, either, but you get my meaning." Blake pushed past annoyance. "Jed is a linchpin. The others respect him. Hell, so do I, but this is one instance where I believe he's made a mistake."

They drove in silence as minutes flowed past. Traffic slowed their pace once they passed the city limits. It appeared many were headed for jobs at this early hour. They passed dozens of likely looking diners, and Blake's stomach rumbled with discontent.

"Told you we should've gotten breakfast," Gideon said. "I'm hungry too."

"How about that bakery over there?" Blake pointed.

"Excellent!" Mac ferried the car to the curb and let it idle while Blake ran inside, returning with several white sacks filled with fresh-baked bread, cinnamon rolls, bear claws, and cookies.

He dropped the bags on the seat between him and Mac. Gideon reached over the front seat's backrest and filched a cinnamon roll studded with nuts and raisins. It smelled delicious, so Blake did the same. He'd bought a lot on purpose, so they wouldn't show up at Jed's empty handed.

"It's the next left," he told Mac.

"Yeah. I remember," his lieutenant said around the oatmeal cookie he was eating.

After two places where they had to double back because none of them recalled exactly how the circuitous streets hung together, they pulled into Jed's driveway. Blake frowned, his nose twitching double-time.

"I smell it too," Gideon said from the backseat. "Started smelling it at the bottom of the hill. How could our mate possibly be inside Jed's house?"

"Let's not sit out here jawing about it." Mac killed the engine and shoved his door open, jumping out.

"Hold up," Blake ordered, raising his voice for emphasis.

"But why?" Gideon was outside the car too. "We need a mate. We've hunted forever."

Blake joined them. "Stop. Just stop. We can't be reacting to Jed's or Les and Karl's mates. The only other woman I know of inside that house isn't mate material."

"Not what my nose says," Mac insisted.

"Or my cock." Gideon patted the tented front of his pants.

Blake got it. He lusted after the woman smell coming from inside. It proclaimed she was available and slated to be theirs. Maybe someone other than whomever Jed had dragged down the mountainside was visiting.

He hoped to hell that was it because, mate bond or not, no way in hell could he bind his family group to anyone related to a Hunter.

"Coming, boss?" Mac sprinted toward ornate front doors with Gideon hot on his heels.

"Yeah, let's at least figure out who she is before we make gloom and doom proclamations," Gideon called.

"If this is as real as it feels—" Mac was almost to the door "—she'll jump our bones before we even cross the lintel."

Blake reached back inside the car and gathered the bakery bags and his keys. "So stay on this side of the door," he told his lieutenant. "I'll be there in a second."

What a shit deal it would be if the woman he hadn't seen up

close and personal in the cave ended up kicking off their mating urge.

It can't be, he argued silently. *I'd have noticed in the Palisades.*

Maybe not. So much death ran free up there, it was all he'd smelled for days.

No help for it. He started for the front door to see exactly what they faced.

CHAPTER 7

Sophie was in the kitchen pouring water and coffee grounds into the huge aluminum percolator. She hadn't slept terribly well. Every time she woke, her fingers found their way between her legs, almost as if once she'd discovered how to pleasure herself, she had to make up for wasted opportunities and years of lost time.

A flash of intense sexual heat threaded from her toes all the way to the top of her head. It stole her breath, and she made a grab for the countertop so she didn't crumple to the floor. What the hell was happening? Had her foray into the forbidden realm of sex kicked some psychic door open where she wouldn't be good for anything else now?

The thought chilled her and she tugged the edges of her power around her, trying to shield herself from the sensations spilling through her. It didn't do any good. The intensity receded fractionally, but for one precarious moment she almost came where she stood.

Alice and Megan rushed through the swinging kitchen doors swathed in robes. Alice wore her typical blue, while Megan's robe was white. Sophie understood she was focusing on small, familiar things to get a grip on a world rapidly catapulting beyond her control.

Thank God she'd had the presence of mind to get dressed before the idea of starting breakfast and surprising everyone had surfaced. She wiped damp hands on her dark, woolen skirt and looked at her friends, not knowing what to say. Telling them her libido had jumped the fence felt far too intimate for the bright, cheerful kitchen with sunlight flooding through the windows over the sink.

"So." Megan faced her and spread her hands wide. "Are you, erm, feeling any different?"

"Not sure what you mean," Sophie hedged.

"What she means is both of us smell a new mate bond forming. Jed, Bron, and Terin rousted me out of bed." Alice chuckled softly. "Not much pries my mates away from me."

"Les and Karl did the same to me," Megan chimed in, her blue eyes glowing with excitement.

"What new mate bond?" Confusion added to Sophie's already heightened emotions.

"Why yours, of course." Alice beamed broadly.

Sophie shook her head, certain she couldn't have heard right. "To whom? So far this morning, I've been in the library and the kitchen. I thought shifters didn't add extra women to their family groups…" Her voice trailed off, and she studied her feet intently. Had her experimentation from the previous night kicked off some magic wherein she was now part of either Alice's or Megan's mate bond? If that happened, how would it work?

"No. Not it at all." Megan strode close and waved a hand in front of Sophie's face. "We're just so excited, we're not being clear. Blake is here. Along with his two lieutenants."

"That's who you're responding to." Alice's words tangled with Megan's. "And maybe that was why none of the men who came by didn't click with you."

"I-I'm sorry." Sophie raked a hand through her hair, realizing she hadn't bothered to braid it this morning and it fell nearly to her knees. Her hands shook as she gathered the thick strands and wound them into a sloppy queue.

"About what?" Megan drew her blonde brows into a straight line. "Alice and I are thrilled."

"What does any of this have to do with the other shifters? It's like you're talking in riddles."

"She's right," Alice said. "I should be ashamed of myself. We're still not being very clear. Blake, Gideon, and Mac are coyote shifters. Maybe your particular brand of magic is a better blend with theirs than with wolf shifters."

Sophie pressed her thighs together. The sexual heat that had assaulted her was still there in force, and she didn't know quite what to do about it. How the hell could she meet men, particularly men who might be her mates—assuming she went in that direction—if she could barely mumble good morning without throwing herself into their arms and plastering her body all over them?

"It will all work out." Megan had obviously been inside her head.

"You'll see." Alice hugged her and looped an arm through hers. "The men are in the study off the main room. Come meet them."

Sophie licked suddenly dry lips. She glanced at herself and her threadbare skirt and the blouse with spots she couldn't quite get out. She'd come with the clothes on her back and had steadfastly turned down the other women's offers of anything beyond a robe to wear while she washed her own clothing. Next she tangled her hands in her uncombed hair.

"Aw shit. I should fix myself up a little."

"It's okay." Megan closed from her other side and hugged her too. "When I met Les and Karl, I'd just spent the night in a barn and I still had straw in my hair."

"And when I met Jed, I'd been climbing for the last twenty hours," Alice said. "I was dirty and sweaty, but the mate bond transcends all that. Come on. Time to meet your prospective mates."

"Is— Is it a done deal?" Sophie was surprised she could get the words out.

"Not necessarily." Alice spoke slowly, clearly picking her words with care. "The sexual attraction will be intense, but you can walk away until you actually mate with them. After that, they can't do whatever it is they do to wipe their memory from your mind."

"They wouldn't have to do that for her," Megan spoke up, "because she already knows what we are."

Alice rolled her eyes. "Yeah, huh? I'm not thinking straight this morning. The guys kept me up most of the night."

Sophie almost said, "I know," but mercifully the words remained on the right side of her lips.

"Come with us." Alice took one arm and Megan the other. Together they drew her through the kitchen and down a long hall lined with priceless art and sculpture, toward the far end of the main floor.

The sound of raised voices reached Sophie long before they saw the men, and she halted precipitously, listening. Alice and Megan still hung onto her, concern streaming from them.

"But she's your mate," Jed protested. "I feel it, so do my boys."

"She can't be," an unfamiliar voice thundered. "From what you said in the Palisades, her brother was a Hunter."

"Sins of the fathers?" Les inquired with a sarcastic inflection.

"I don't fucking care what you call it," the unfamiliar voice continued. "We don't need her kind."

"You're being hasty, boss," a second unfamiliar voice jumped into the fray.

"Stop. Just stop," Jed said. Sharp-toned anger ran beneath his words. "Good God, Blake. That bit you said about not needing her kind made my blood run cold. Listen to yourself, brother. It's the same shit people have said about us."

"I don't care," the first unfamiliar voice insisted. "We showed up early because I needed to talk with you—about her as well as other things. This mate thing is unexpected, unneeded, and unwelcome."

Still locked between Alice and Megan, Sophie felt tears well. These men didn't want her. No reason to face the pain and humiliation of marching into the room, even for the satisfaction of telling them they were a bunch of dicks.

She wrenched away from her friends and bolted for the nearest stairwell, running until her chest ached from not breathing fast enough to support her headlong flight. Tears poured down her face, blinding her. When she got to her room, she flung the door open, fell inside, and slammed and locked it behind her, sobbing helplessly.

Through it all, the goddamned, fucking sexual heat still dogged her. Would it ever go away? Would she be stuck with it forever, so long as Blake and his men were here? Jesus, but she wished she knew more.

She pushed the glass door open, welcoming the rush of cool air on her overheated face and body. Maybe she couldn't stay in her room forever, but it beat the living hell out of facing the bunch downstairs, feeling their pity—and their scorn. Yeah, Abe had been a Hunter, but that was his choice, not hers. White-hot anger at being judged raced along her nerve endings, but it was a pleasant counterpart to her sorrow of a few moments before.

Sitting was out of the question, so she paced from one side of the room to the other acutely aware of the three coyote shifters two floors down. Her gaze skittered back to the open door. Maybe she could solve everyone's problems and climb down from the balcony.

Sophie went outside and threw her magic wide open, listening intently. Her room was at the far end of the house, but she could still hear the men's voices raised in argument, punctuated from time to time by Alice and Megan, sounding equally furious. Bending over the ornate iron railing, she glanced down. An evergreen grew close, but not near enough to make things easy. If she could just get to the tree, she'd have it made. Shinnying down it would be simple, and then she could head for the main road and put out her thumb.

Someone would pick her up.

The shifters would be hopping mad if they caught her, so she needed to move fast. She piled on all the clothes she'd arrived in and hurriedly braided her hair. It didn't take long. Back on the balcony, she looked at what she had to work with. It would be dicey, but her balance was good. She'd need to get her feet on the balcony's railing, reach for the uneven stonework that made up the mansion's exterior walls, and walk herself to the tree. The nearest branch was only about six feet away. Even if it broke under her weight, she could use it to lever herself into the main part of the tree.

Heart pounding, Sophie didn't give herself time to rethink things. She swung her body up onto the railing and crawled her fingers up the stones until she found an inch-wide ledge. It gave her enough leverage to get her feet under her. Finding another protrusion big enough to toe across was harder. A breath-stealing moment later, she reached for and caught a higher ledge. It gave her toes purchase on something that didn't stick out more than pencil width, but it was the best she was likely to get. With a final glance at the safety of her little patio two feet below, she moved toward the tree.

The first two steps were fine, but then the upper ledge vanished. No matter where she scrabbled with her fingertips, nothing else met her frantic groping. The tree was close. In a final, desperate move, she pushed off with her feet and flew through the air, arms flailing as she grabbed at needles and branches flashing past. When she was certain she'd fall to the ground and break something, one of her arms latched around a tree limb and held.

Gasping and panting, she pushed toward the main trunk. She wanted to howl, scream, but she had to keep going. Her arms and legs shook from adrenaline coursing through her, but at least the sexual tension had dissipated.

She bit back wry laughter. Good to know survival still trumped sex.

The last few feet went easily, and she'd never felt anything quite so welcome as the ground beneath her booted feet. Taking care to make as little noise as possible, she drew Native magic to blend with the trees and shrubs and made her way around the house. Once she hit the long driveway, she broke into a run, casting a resigned glance at her car sitting on blocks. Karl was in the midst of fixing it. Too bad. If it was running, she'd have had a much readier escape route, just no money for gas.

Never mind about the car. The goddess was looking out for me because I escaped.

Not home free quite yet, sister.

After a car picks me up, then I can relax.

A car meant she had to pick a direction. Not north. Big Pine would be the first place they'd look for her. No, east into the desert was her best chance. Maybe she could lose herself in some of the fancy casinos in Las Vegas. They were always hiring show-girls. She'd never been much of a dancer, but how hard could it be?

As she put distance between herself and Jed's mansion, she thought about the men she'd sensed but never seen, and a perva-sive sadness filled her. For a pathetically short time, she'd deluded herself she could have a normal life. At least normal by shifter standards, but they didn't want her, either.

Don't think about it. Just keep moving. If I don't, I'll turn around and everything I did to get out of there will have been for nothing.

BLAKE STORMED over to double glass doors fronting on a small garden, turned the latch, and pushed hard. Far from ending things, his staunch refusal to even consider the Hunter's sister had earned him censure from everyone. His lieutenants had retreated to a corner of the spacious study, backs turned to him as they conversed privately.

Jed, Bron, and Terin grew progressively angrier, as did Les and Karl. But the worst were their mates. Alice and Megan had apparently taken Sophie under their wing. They saw her as a friend—as if anyone even remotely connected to a Hunter could be considered a friend to anyone—and they'd laid into him too.

Outside, away from the turmoil and drama, he breathed deep and forced his limbs into motion, beating a circular path through the garden. At least the hideous sexual heat had receded, giving him a chance to think. Mac and Gideon's accusations stung. They'd called him a racist and a bigot, right along with Jed. And the women's account of Sophie falling apart, bolting for the stairs, and sobbing piteously hadn't helped.

One thing was certain, he had fences to repair. A battle loomed on the horizon, one big enough to blot out the sun for their kind. For them to devolve into petty power struggles right now could truly ring the death knell for shifters. They were long-lived and healed fast, but they were far from immortal.

Once the first flush of anger passed, the place inside him that burned with loneliness asserted its presence. His family group had been mateless for so long, he'd given up on ever finding a woman to grace their home. After they moved from the Old Country, the odds grew even worse. He was resigned to that fate—more or less —but his lieutenants weren't. Not that he didn't recognize the rush of sensuality from earlier as raw material for the mate bond, but just because it was there didn't force them to accept the woman.

Far from it.

He stopped pacing. No reason to waste any more energy on this. What he needed to do was smooth the waters. He'd just turned to head back inside the house when Alice and Megan burst through the double doors.

"I hope you're happy with yourself." Alice raised a fist and shook it at him.

"Sophie was so excited to meet you, and you destroyed her," Megan spoke over Alice. "You have no idea what she's gone through, what kind of life she led. Her Hunter brother—the one you're all fussed up over—well he raped her when she was just a kid. And kept on raping her for years."

"She hated him," Jed broke in, and Blake saw that the men had piled outside too.

"Fine." He spread his hands in front of him. "It's unfortunate she was ill-treated. Maybe I was hasty—"

"No shit," Gideon stomped over to him. "Thanks to you, she's gone."

Blake drew back, shocked. "Gone? What do you mean, gone?"

"She was so anxious to get away from another man who hated her—" Alice pushed right in front of him, inches from his face, "—she went out the window."

"Lucky our mate didn't break her neck," Mac cut in, "but Gid and I are going after her. We want her, even if you don't." He turned and raced around the house with Gideon right behind him.

Blake opened his mouth, but words eluded him. Both his lieutenants had just engaged in clear insubordination. He should sprint after them, employ magic to force them to stay, but somehow he knew it would only make matters worse. The sound of a car engine racing before it had warmed up told him Mac and Gideon were burning rubber down the driveway.

"We're going after her too," Jed latched his blue eyes onto Blake's.

Something hard and brittle inside him shattered and guilt burned bright, followed by shame. He'd been a dick and now look what had happened. "I'll help," he said.

"Yeah," Les sneered. "Only because you're afraid she'll finger us."

Blake shook his head. "No. Because what I did was wrong. If something happens to her because she ends up getting into the wrong car, I'll have to live with myself for a long time. Just because I spurned the mate bond doesn't mean I want her dead. Not anymore."

Bron hit him with a splash of magic that stung. "Son of a bitch. You're telling the truth."

Jed cast a meaningful glance at his lieutenant. "He outranks you. Watch it."

"Let's go," Terin said. "Every minute we waste, Sophie's trail gets that much colder."

"Megan and I are coming." Alice faced off against her mate.

"Of course you are, sweetheart." Jed flashed her a tired smile. "Never doubted it for a moment."

Everyone bolted for the driveway and sorted themselves into two cars. Blake went with Alice, Jed, and his two lieutenants. Megan and her mates piled into the other car. Terin ended up in the backseat with Blake. The red-haired shifter turned to him. "What's wrong with you, brother?"

"Same thing I told Bron applies to you too," Jed shot from the driver's seat as he catapulted down the long, curving driveway.

"Sorry," Terin muttered. "Rephrasing that—"

"Don't bother." Blake curled his upper lip, feeling his canines lengthen. He got hold of the animal side of his nature fast. Shifting in the car wouldn't do anyone any good. "I reacted. Anything Hunter turns my stomach."

"But she isn't. She hates them too," Alice said from her spot between Jed and Bron.

"How do you know?" Blake was surprised he was even asking. He wanted to get past anything associated with Sophie, and if getting her back where Alice and Megan could cluck over her would accomplish that, he was all for it.

"We've tested her nine ways from Sunday with our magic," Jed replied. "If she had any sympathy for those bastards, we'd have figured it out by now."

"This isn't a good time to be focused on mating," Blake blustered, wanting to change the subject to the threat they faced.

"Jesus!" Bron twisted from where he sat and stared over the backrest. "Anytime any of us finds a potential mate, it's cause to rejoice."

"Enough," Jed snapped. "Sophie is a good woman. Sparing her life was a sound choice. If we sink into mindless killing, we may as well sign on with the Hunters."

The wolf clan's alpha had a point, but Blake had been mired in survival mode for so long, his focus had grown narrow. He grimaced inwardly. Maybe after they located Sophie, he'd humor his lieutenants and at least get all of them in the same room together. That ought to mollify Gideon and Mac, and then they could get down to the real business of killing more Hunters to ensure their own survival.

CHAPTER 8

Sophie stood on the shoulder of Route 66 with her thumb out. Cars whizzed past. She shook out her hair and tried to look like someone a person might want to help. She was thirsty, but there wasn't any help for that. She was damned if she'd return to the cluster of stores a quarter mile back where she might get a glass of water. Eyeing the angle of the sun, she calculated a couple hours had passed since she pelted down Jed's driveway. Luckily the highway wasn't too far, and a penny bus ride had both shielded her—in case anyone discovered her absence—and saved her several miles walking.

She rattled the few coins in her pocket. Maybe fifty cents total. It wasn't enough for much, but if she could just get to Barstow, where a different road cut northeast to Las Vegas, she'd look for something to drink there. Realizing she was staring at her feet, she forced herself to stand straight and pasted a pleasant smile on her face. Sure enough, a dark blue sedan braked and slowed, rolling to a stop next to her.

The car's sole occupant, a man, reached across to roll down the passenger window. "Where you headed, girly?"

Sophie stared at him, doing her damnedest to assess if he was a threat. She reached out threads of magic, but they didn't yield anything.

"Guess you're not wanting a ride after all." The man, maybe forty with thinning brown hair and close-set brown eyes began rolling up the window. His pressed, white shirt was open at the collar, and the cuffs were folded back.

"No!" She hurried to the side of the car. "Wait. It's just I was hoping for maybe a family to ride with."

"No family." He raised his upper lip, showing tobacco-stained teeth. "Just me. Make up your mind, girly. I ain't got all day."

Now that she was closer, she scented the same tobacco that had yellowed his teeth, but at least there wasn't any liquor smell. "Are you headed to Barstow," she asked.

He nodded once curtly. "Past there too. All the way across the country."

Something about him bothered her, but she'd been standing by the side of the highway for close to half an hour, and he was the first one who'd given her a second glance. She had to get moving, otherwise Jed and the group of shifters would surely track her location. If it came down to it, she could always open the door and jump out. She might get bruised up a little, but—"

"Time's up." He cranked the window.

Sophie gripped the handle and pulled the door open. "I'd love a ride. Thank you."

"Mmph." He made a grunting noise. "You always take this long to figure things out?"

"Sorry." She ginned up an apologetic smile. "I'm just tired."

He looked behind him and pulled back onto the highway. When he didn't try to engage her in conversation, Sophie thought maybe things might be all right. It wasn't that far to Barstow. They'd be there before nightfall. Hopefully, it'd be warm enough for her to curl up beneath some trees. Hitchhiking after dark felt riskier, though that probably wasn't true.

"Here." He thrust an open bottle of soda her way. "Want some?"

She took it, and an unpleasant zing shocked her. Sophie maintained a neutral expression. Her magic had just sounded a warning. Was there something wrong with the cola?

"Ain't you gonna drink it?" The man sent a look her way, sly and calculating wrapped up into one unpleasant package.

"I'm not really thirsty." She pushed it back his way. Instead of drinking, he dropped it into a bottle holder bolted to his door.

"Have it your way, girly. I'm just trying to be nice."

"I'm sure you are."

They lapsed into silence as they cleared the outskirts of Los Angeles. Desert stretched around them, empty and silent. Route 66 had opened a dozen years before, and was extremely popular as a cross-country route, but today only a few cars traversed its broad lanes. After they'd been underway for about an hour, the man, who'd never bothered to give her his name, slowed and turned off onto a dirt road.

Sophie's stomach tightened. "Where are we going?"

"Nature call. Bet you probably need one too."

Peeing was the last thing on her mind, especially after the man kept driving. She reached for the door handle, intent on escape, and couldn't find one. Only a stub where it had once attached. Her heart slammed into panic mode and bile, hot and burning, splashed the back of her throat.

Shit! The son of a bitch locked me in.

Every thwarted instinct she'd swallowed all the times Abe took her against her will raced to the fore. No way in hell would she go down without a fight. Never again.

Because he was focused on the rutted road and keeping his tires out of deep divots, she was able to remove the knife in her thigh sheath without him noticing what she was about. Once she had it in hand, she tucked it out of sight beneath her, ready to strike as soon as she got a chance.

What if he doesn't give me that chance?

I'll just have to make my own.

"You should've had some of that soda," he said nastily.

"Why?" She tried to sound mildly curious rather than scared out of her wits.

"Would've made this next part go down easier." He pulled the car to a stop and killed the engine. Jumping down, he came around to her side and pulled her door open. "Get out." Mistaking her hesitation for refusal, he drew a pistol from one of his pockets and waved it at her. "Get going. Now."

She jumped down, ignoring the running board, and kept the knife first behind her and then on the side facing away from him. Sophie took shallow breaths through her mouth. She had to stay calm, not react too soon. He was bigger than her. Stronger. And his gun was a long range weapon, compared with her up-close-and-personal knife. If she showed her hand too soon, he'd take the knife away, and then she truly would be in deep trouble. Even worse than where she was right now.

He came around to her. "You know what comes next, girly. Your kind always does. This can go down easy or hard. Your choice."

She forced herself to smile. "I don't understand."

"Like hell you don't." He gripped her shoulders with one hand and mauled her breasts with the other.

She grunted in pain and noticed his breathing escalated. Aw shit. He was one of those like Abe. He liked it rough. Rough turned him on. She had to get him close enough to drive her blade into something that would kill him. More acid splashed the back of her throat, and fury hazed her vision, but she held herself back.

Not yet.

In an out and out contest, she was strong for a woman, but she'd still lose.

He let go of her breasts long enough to unzip his pants and pull out his already erect cock. It stank when he pulled back the foreskin, and she recoiled, but his harsh grip on her shoulder held her in place.

"Pull up them skirts and lay on your back," he grunted through rising excitement. He stroked himself just like Abe used to do, and she wanted to puke all over him. Letting go of his death grip on her shoulder, he pushed her downward.

Getting him on top of her would work. When he was lost in rut, she'd kill him. And stab him a few extra times for Abe too.

Sophie dropped to her knees at the same time as she let the knife fall behind her, hoping one sound would cancel the other out. The man was busy jacking himself and watching her with hot, little eyes. She arranged her body so she could get to her weapon and pulled her skirts up.

"Take them knickers off, or I'll rip 'em to shreds."

She tugged her panties out of the way and steeled herself for the press of his dick. Every instinct she had screamed to run, but he'd shoot her if she did. Who knew what kind of marksman he was? Hell, he'd shoot her as soon as he was done. He couldn't afford to let her live and report him to the authorities. She was only an Indian, but rape was still against the law.

Sophie forced herself to keep her eyes open. With Abe, she'd always glued them shut.

The man hunkered between her spread legs, getting an eyeful, while still working his cock. From the looks of things, he'd come in seconds, so she'd have to be fast. He lunged between her thighs, burying himself in one stroke. He reared back long enough to spit, "I knew you weren't no virgin. Sluts, all of you Indian bitches."

After that, he got down to business.

Sophie reached under herself and gripped the knife. He was gasping and panting now, hips pumping as fast as he could. His eyes were closed. She reached around him to get a two handed grip on her knife and plunged it deep into the side of his neck, calling on her power to help her, make her strong enough to prevail. He started to react when she reached around him, but before he could emerge from the sexual hunger holding him in thrall, it was too late.

She jimmied out from under him and held the knife deep, slicing sideways to make certain she severed the major vessels in his neck. Murderous rage replaced the lust in his eyes. He reached for her neck, intent on choking the life from her, seconds before blood shot into the air when she hit an artery. After one hard squeeze, his hands fell to the sand, useless, and Sophie shrieked her triumph while doing her best to avoid being splattered with blood.

She was still screeching like a madwoman when the blood quit geysering. Taking a good look at the man's glazed eyes, she knew he was on his way out. *Good!* One less perverted bastard to prey on women like her. His comment about Indian women being sluts infuriated her. How many others had he lured into his car, raped, and killed? Her magic might give her the answer, so long as she kept a hand on his body, but she didn't want to know. The others were just as dead as she would've been.

She yanked hard on her knife to extract it and cleaned it and her hands with sand and the bottom part of the man's trousers. It was excruciating to touch him, but she wanted to slip the knife back out of sight. Having the man's blood on her was worse than touching the hem of his trousers. Scrambling to her feet, she retrieved her underwear, slithered into it, and took stock as she sheathed her knife.

Keys. If she could find the car keys, she could drive out of there. She'd dump the car as soon as she got close to Barstow. Figure out a way to clean the rest of his blood off herself and keep going. No way could she tell the authorities she'd murdered a white man. They'd never believe he attacked her first. Indians weren't high on anyone's list of innocent victims. Even reporting him for rape wouldn't have been a sure thing. It might be against the law, but no one had listened when she complained about what Abe did to her.

The faint hum of an engine nicked the edges of her hearing. Funny. She hadn't been able to hear Route 66 before. Sophie stood stock still and funneled power into listening. *Damn.* Could things get any worse? A car, actually more than one, was travelling straight for her, kicking up dust in their wake.

Was it a bunch of men heading out into the desert to shoot deer and get drunk?

She glanced at the man's coated-in-blood body. No matter if she found the keys, there wasn't a way to explain what she was doing all the way out here with a corpse. The sagebrush wasn't high enough or thick enough to hide either herself or the man. She had to do something fast, and the only option was her magic. Summoning the ability to blend in with nature, she ran to the car long enough to snatch the keys out of the ignition. If she got really lucky, whoever was coming wouldn't stay. Once they saw the body, they'd make a run for the nearest town to alert someone. It would give her an escape window.

She curved her hands into fists. *Goddammit.* She hadn't come this far to fail.

Sophie retreated about fifty yards from the car and hunkered behind the largest sagebrush plant she could find. Humming a spell, she wove strands of invisibility about her, creating the illusion she was just another bush. To lessen the odds of stray sunbeams illuminating the silver streaks in her hair, she tugged her hood over her head and waited, scarcely breathing.

She was dangerously close to the end of her reserves. Could she maintain her illusion long enough for whoever it was to stop, take a look at the dead man, and skedaddle out of there? Maybe they wouldn't stop at all, but that seemed remote, what with the man's car sitting off to the side of the dirt road.

Sophie focused on the dirt beneath her boot soles, asking every mother goddess to shield her, protect her. The cars—she'd determined there were three—moved inexorably closer, but she couldn't shift her attention away from her spell. Hell, she couldn't alter her concentration enough to wish them well and truly gone.

One of the cars stopped. Doors flew open and footsteps pounded her way.

Goddammit!

Eyes shut, drowning in fear until breathing became a struggle, she repeated, *They can't see me*, to herself over and over. The other cars stopped too. The sound of more doors opening battered her.

"Sophie!" Alice's voice cried. "It's going to be okay. Come on out, hon!"

"Aw Jesus. This guy's dead," Bron's voice yelled. "Get over here, Terin, and help me with him."

Sophie's spell frittered away, shattering as her concentration fled. Could this be right? Was she hallucinating because she'd killed a man? Her friends couldn't possibly have found her.

Why not? They're excellent trackers.

Aw shit. Not friends. I was their prisoner. What will they do to me?

The boots thudding toward her grew closer. Unfamiliar men's voices called out directional changes. Because she'd rather face defeat standing than cowering, Sophie opened her eyes and pushed to her feet just as two men closed on her. One had coal black hair and equally dark eyes. The other's hair was a brilliant red, and he nailed her with a grim set of hazel eyes.

"Thank fucking God." The redhead closed his arms around her, crushing her against him so close the beat of his heart thudded against her ear.

The same sexual heat that had bombarded her in Jed's house started in the soles of her feet, surrounding her with such intense sensation, she pressed her body close to the stranger's and felt her nipples pebble into points of need.

Alice and Megan pushed the redhead aside and closed their arms around her crooning. "I'm just so sorry, hon," Megan murmured.

"You're not mad because I ran away?" Sophie's voice came out as a squeak.

"Hell, no. Meg and I don't blame you. Blake was an asshole." Alice tightened her grip on Sophie's shoulders. "You gave me such a fright when I went to your room and realized you'd jumped out your window." Drawing back, she fastened her green eyes on Sophie. "Don't ever do that again. Okay? I know you were devastated, but Meg and I are here for you. You can always talk with us."

Alice's tenderness undid Sophie. The fear and tension from the past few hours caught up, and her throat thickened with emotion. Tears spilled over, dripping down her face.

"It's okay. Cry." Megan patted her arm. "You have every right to. My God. You risked falling to your death, and then that bastard who picked you up must've been a piece of shit. What'd he do?"

"Tried to rape me." Sophie got the words out between sobs. She jerked her chin defiantly. "But I got him good. He'll never, never stick his cock into another unwilling woman. I got him for Abe. For all those times I was helpless. Well, I'm not helpless anymore. I'm glad I killed him. I'd do it again." She snuffled. "I'm babbling. Don't mind me."

The two men who'd reached her first were joined by a third. This one had blond hair with coppery highlights and aquamarine eyes. He looked from Megan to Alice to Sophie, and it seemed he was struggling to find something to say.

Alice saved him the trouble. "This is Blake." She pointed at the newcomer. "He's alpha for the coyote clan. The others are Gideon —" she motioned to the dark-haired man "—and Mac, Blake's lieutenants."

Sophie stiffened, snuffling back tears as she remembered the discussion that had driven her first to her room and then out of Jed's mansion. Her body was on fire with wanting the men standing close to her, but she ignored the sensations cascading through her.

"I'm fine," she said tightlipped, addressing her words to Blake. "I don't need your pity. You don't have to have anything to do with me. Not now. Not ever." Before she did something to belie her words, like throwing herself back into Mac's arms, she turned away and began walking toward where she'd left the dead man.

"Wait." Blake moved lightning fast, so his body blocked her path.

"Why should I?" She leveled her gaze at him. "I've had a hell of a day, and I'm not in the mood for whatever crap you want to throw my way."

Megan latched an arm through Alice's. "We'll be just over there if you need us," she told Sophie.

"You might want to hear whatever Blake has to say," Alice suggested with a knowing smile. "He may have come to his senses on the drive out here. God knows the bunch of us jumped his shit long enough and hard enough."

Sophie stood tall and gazed at Blake. She pushed her hood back until it rested on her shoulders. "I'm not interested in anything you had to be talked into."

Mac and Gideon drew close. "Blake's our alpha, but we never agreed with him about you," Gideon said, his dark eyes alight with something untamed.

"We left Jed's as soon as we knew you were gone," Mac added. "Without Blake. Gid and I discussed it and decided we wanted to give what we felt for you a fair shot, even if our alpha wasn't on board."

"I don't quite understand." Sophie looked from one man to the next. "How would that have worked?"

"Badly," Blake said succinctly.

He reached a hand to her, but she ignored it, bringing a sardonic grin to his face.

Christ but he was good-looking. Sophie found herself staring before she realized what she was doing and looked away. The smile lit his eyes from within, and made him movie star handsome.

"You're not going to make this easy on me," Blake said, "and I don't blame you. I was a total ass."

"Good you see that," Gideon muttered.

Sophie looked from one man to the next before glancing back at the collection of cars. Jed and the other men had come up with a shovel, and they were busy digging a grave.

Adrenaline from killing her assailant was fading, and she swayed on her feet. Mac reached for her, but she waved him off.

Both the other men were looking pointedly at Blake. "This isn't easy for me," he began. "I'm a military strategist, not a lover, but I accept complete responsibility for what happened to you today." He trained the full impact of his unusual eyes right on her. "I'm impressed by your courage. I was wrong about your blood ties to a Hunter tainting you, and I apologize for the things I said earlier."

"Goddammit, boss," Mac muttered. "Your thoughtless comments forced her to kill. Never mind risking her neck climbing down from her third floor balcony."

"You think I don't know that?" Blake swung to face his lieutenant. "I feel like warmed over shit that I shoved down my own gullet, but there's nothing I can do to take back what I said."

He focused on her again. "I don't expect you to forgive me anytime soon, but I'll hold out hope we can get past our rocky beginning."

"If you were willing to accept the mate bond, you could begin by mating with us," Mac said, his eyes glittering with hope and desire.

"We wouldn't have to add Blake in right away," Gideon chimed in.

Desire for the men standing in front of her flared, flickered, and died as the feel of the man she'd killed rooting away on her filled her mind.

"I—I can't." She looked away. "It's too soon."

Understanding softened Blake's stark features. "Aw Jesus, God, that man actually raped you?" At her mute nod, his face darkened. "If he wasn't already dead, I'd hunt him down and rip his neck from his body. When you were talking with the women you said he tried. Why'd you let him get that close?"

Defiance stiffened her spine. "I had a knife. He had a gun. I had to catch him off his guard—and get him close enough to kill him."

Blake bent from the waist and bowed, admiration richly evident in the courtly, old world gesture. "I'm in awe of your strength and your courage."

His words warmed her. That someone actually understood the hell she'd lived through and respected her actions meant the world.

Mac and Gideon inclined their heads too. "We'll wait for you to decide about us and the mate bond," Mac said.

"As long as it takes," Gideon cut in. "Now let us take you back to Jed's."

"That would be wonderful. I feel dirty inside. Maybe standing under a hot shower until it runs cold will help."

"If that happens, we'll heat water on the stove until you tell us you don't want any more," Blake said, his tone laced with sincerity.

Amazed she could still walk, Sophie turned and wended her way around rocks and sagebrush. Once she got to the collection of vehicles, Mac and Gideon herded her into their car. After a hurried conference with Jed, Blake got behind the wheel.

"We're not going to wait for the others," he told her. "They'll finish burying the body and drive the car a long way off the road. Somewhere it's less likely to be noticed. They'll pull the plates off it too and lose them elsewhere in the desert."

Sophie dug deep into a pocket and held out a set of keys. "Here."

Gideon whistled. "Yeah, guess those would help. I'll deliver them to Jed, and we can be on our way."

Alice trotted to the car and bent to stick her head in an open window. "Once you're cleaned up," she said, "help yourself to whatever you want in my closet. Your clothes have blood all over them."

"Oh, I couldn't—" Sophie began.

"You can and you will," Alice insisted.

"When you're feeling better," Blake said, "maybe you'll let one of us take you shopping. I understand from Jed you left all your things at your home in Big Pine."

"Yeah, I did leave my clothes, but that's a *no* on you doing anything for me." She tried to sound firm, but her voice trembled a little. "I don't want to be beholden to anyone."

"We hope you'll become our mate." Gideon smiled softly. "It would be an honor and a privilege to take care of you."

"I've been taking care of myself for a long time," she countered.

"Just because something's always been a certain way," Blake said as he started the car and fiddled with the controls to adjust the gas mixture, "is no reason it can't change."

$\mathcal{B}$lake kept a close eye on Sophie. She'd fallen asleep once they hit Route 66 and its smooth pavement. Sandwiched in the front seat between him and Gideon, she slumped against the seat cushions. Dark circles etched beneath her eyes, and a savage protectiveness shot through him. She hadn't had time to recover from the carnage in the Palisades, and his stupidity had forced her from the safe haven Jed tried to provide.

"Jesus, I've been worse than a fool." He directed his mind voice to his lieutenants. *"Thanks for not beating me up worse over it."*

"You're an exceptional leader for our clan," Gideon said.

"But it's an art that requires decisiveness, not compassion," Mac observed. *"You were just being your usual pig-headed, single-minded self earlier today."*

"Yeah, you had no idea she'd overhear," Gideon added.

"Wouldn't have mattered if I knew she was on the other side of the door." Blake was brutally honest. *"I believed what I said at the time, but that was before I knew anything about her."*

"And now?" Mac quirked a brow. Blake caught his expression in the rear view mirror.

"Now I'm ashamed of myself. She's the bravest woman I've ever met. Her spirit must be made of plate steel to have lived through everything she has and still have the moxie to fight back. She lured that man with her body, knowing she'd sink her knife in him. Not many men would be able to do that."

"There's a reason the mate bond shows up when it does," Gideon's mind voice was slow, cautious.

"True," Mac agreed. *"It's not random. If it were, we'd have found lots of possibilities for mates over the years. Instead of none."*

"And here I figured we were still alone because coyotes are such a cantankerous lot. Always running in packs and killing things." Blake tried to joke.

"Wolves aren't any different," Gideon noted archly.

"Oh yes, they are," Mac said. *"Wolves form bonds with humans. Coyotes are too smart for that."*

"Don't let Jed hear you say that," Blake cautioned. *"Or those lieutenants of his, or Les and Karl."*

"Pot. Kettle." Gideon chortled softly. *"The one who can't keep his mouth shut handing out sage advice."*

Blake glanced at Sophie and paid out a dollop of shifter magic to keep her asleep. Her body must ache from her headlong flight and whatever the man did to her. Somehow he figured they still didn't have the whole story, but he'd be damned if he'd grill her. If she wanted or needed to talk, he'd lend an ear. Otherwise, he wanted her to move beyond the horrors of today.

He thought about the meeting tomorrow night. Keir and Jon would show up, along with their lieutenants. What if Sophie agreed to the mate bond, only to have it blow up in front of her when war escalated and shifters were forced into a direct confrontation that would mean many deaths?

He reined in the grim edges of his imagination. No way to control the future. Maybe Sophie would accept the mate bond. Maybe not. He had to find out if Alice and Megan had described exactly what it entailed. Even if they had, it was still a conversation he, Mac, and Gideon needed to have with Sophie, so she could weigh the pros and cons.

"Do you want to stop for groceries before we get home?" Gideon asked softly.

Blake shook his head. "No. If our mate needs something one of us can go out for it later. I want to get her to Jed's."

Gideon lowered his eyebrows and reverted to telepathy. *"Oh, so she's our mate now?"*

Surprise washed through Blake, but he'd actually said that. Protectiveness, feral and savage burned in his chest. Even if Sophie didn't want him, he'd yearn for her for the rest of his days.

"He does seem to be warming to the idea," Mac murmured from the backseat.

"Shut up." Blake caught his eye in the mirror. *"I'm going to do everything I can to make things up to her. Meantime, have either of you caught wind of anything on the radio about our mountain killing spree?"*

"When would we have had a chance?" Mac asked.

Blake reached for the knob to turn the radio on, but drew his hand back before he touched it. He wanted information, but wasn't willing to disturb the woman slumbering next to him. Her needs came first from now on. More than anything, that told him the mate bond had him in thrall.

That and his painfully hard cock pressing against the buttons of his pants. The scents of lust and hunger filled the car, which didn't help things. No matter what, they wouldn't press her. She had to come to them, and even if she did, they'd take things slow. The only thing men had dished her way was misery.

By God, he'd change all that. Pleasing her had just moved to the very top of his list. He'd figure out how to slot everything else in—and some of his duties to the coyote clan might suffer a little —but Sophie would never, never get short shrift from him again.

Almost as if she'd been privy to his thoughts, she stirred in her magically deepened sleep, and her full lips parted in a ghost of a smile.

~

SOPHIE WOKE to night spilling through the open drapes of her room at Jed's mansion. The men had walked her inside, with Blake running ahead. By the time Mac and Gideon accompanied her up two flights of stairs to her room—assistance she'd been clear she didn't need—Blake had started water running in the deep, claw foot tub in the gleaming white marble bathroom adjacent to where she slept.

Anxiety that they'd try to do something had tightened her gut, but when they left her, shutting the door behind them, disappointment followed in their wake. Part of her hoped they'd return. Another part wanted to be alone. Regardless—who knew, perhaps they sensed her ambivalence—no one had bothered her. When she returned to her room, scrubbed and with wet hair trailing down her back, someone had left clothes folded at the end of her bed.

She hadn't bothered to dress. Just removed her thick, terry cloth robe and laid down. At first, she feared visions of what she'd done would haunt her, keep her awake. Rather than remorse, grim satisfaction filled her. She'd finally stood up for herself, and having done it once, she had no doubt she could do it again. She'd crossed a line today. Moved from victim to independence, and it felt good.

Damned good.

Falling asleep hadn't been a problem.

She stretched and moved to a cross-legged sit on the bed. A faint tap sounded on the door, followed by Alice's voice. "You up, hon?"

"Yeah. Come on in."

Sophie reached for her discarded robe and slipped it on.

Alice smiled from the doorway, illuminated in light from the hall. "We waited for you. Come on down and eat with us."

"Aw, you shouldn't have. It's late."

"Nah, only eight or so. Jed and the boys and I often don't have dinner until now. We get so caught up in each other, time gets away from us, but we sure do work up an appetite." Rich laughter followed her words, warming Sophie from the inside out.

"Give me a few. I need to brush out my hair. Since I slept on it wet, it might take me a while."

"No problem. Here." Alice moved into the room and laid an armful of clothing across what was already on the bed. "Good to have choices. In case you didn't like what I left earlier, here're a few more things."

"You're awfully kind." Sophie fingered soft cotton and flicked on the overhead lights so she could get a better look.

"Want me to work on your hair?" Alice asked. Without waiting for an answer, she plucked a brush from the highboy dresser and stood behind Sophie, starting at the bottom and working tangles out of her thick, heavy locks.

Sophie leaned into her touch. "No one's pampered me since I was a child."

"I'd say it's long overdue. You have the most gorgeous hair. Have the silver streaks always been there?"

"Yup. Ever since I was a little girl. You have no idea how much teasing I got over being one of the Old Ones." She took a breath. "It's from my magic. That's how it marks some of us."

"Interesting." Alice moved higher, separating sections as she finished them. "You'll have to talk with Megan. She had quite the experience with Cree up in Canada."

"You'd mentioned that. I haven't had a chance to sit down with her since that first night in Mojave, and then we talked about the mate bond and how entranced she is by Les and Karl."

"The men will be closeted in meetings tomorrow night. Might be a good time for another girl gab fest. There." Alice set the brush down. "Not perfect, but good enough."

"A gab fest sounds like fun." Sophie shook her head back and forth, feeling her hair settle around her. "I usually braid it, but I'll keep it loose tonight." She began rooting through the clothes Alice brought, selecting a dark green skirt and an ivory blouse with a matching ivory cardigan that felt as if it had been loomed from cashmere.

"You'll drive the men crazy with your hair down." Alice took a step back, eyeing her appraisingly. "You're a knockout with it up, but down softens the bone structure in your face."

Sophie's cheeks heated at the unexpected compliment. "Thanks. I kind of hate to put my boots on. Do you suppose anyone would mind if I were barefoot?"

"I sure wouldn't." Alice linked an arm through hers. "And we're off."

"Thanks for coming to get me. I am hungry."

"We all figured you would be." Alice hesitated. "I'm not prodding, but if you ever need to talk about what happened today, Meg and I are good listeners."

"At least for now, I'm okay. In a lot of ways, today closed a circle. I may have done murder, but I found myself, if that makes sense."

"It does. Clearing the slate. Maybe it needed to happen before you bond yourself to the coyote clan."

Sophie stopped dead on the second floor landing. "Now just a minute," she sputtered. "I'm a long way from making up my mind about that."

Alice fixed steely, green eyes on her. "Keep deluding yourself, honey. Once a shifter family group stakes their claim to you, there's only one way out. And it's a humdinger. You'll never be sorry, and you'll never look back."

As if Alice's words had loosed a dam, sexual sensation spilled through Sophie with a pull an inexorable as the tide. "Dinner first."

"Oh yeah." Alice's generous mouth stretched into a knowing grin. "Definitely dinner first."

Sophie walked into the dining room with its richly carved

wainscoting with a dry throat and breasts heavy with need. A scrabble of chairs as the men stood amused her. No one had ever stood up when she came into a room before. Blake, Gideon, and Mac sprinted toward her and bumped against one another as they herded her to a seat near the far end of the table.

"For Christ's sake." Jed rolled his eyes. "You'll suffocate the lady. Give her some breathing room."

"We don't tell you how to behave around your mate," Blake rounded on him.

Sophie opened her mouth to protest that she was far from their mate, to reiterate nothing had been decided, but the words refused to emerge. Flustered, she settled her napkin across her lap and grabbed her wine goblet.

"Before you drink," Blake said, "I'd like to propose a toast." He settled into the seat next to her. Gideon sat on her other side, and Mac directly across from her.

"Here, here," Mac chimed in, raising his glass. "To Sophie."

Her eyes widened in shock. They were toasting her. "For what?" Confused, she gazed from one person to the next all down the long table.

"Being a survivor, honey." Megan tipped her chin at a jaunty angle. "Takes one to know one."

Everyone tipped their glasses back as, "To Sophie," echoed through the room.

Heat clawed from her chest up over the top of her head, and she figured she was blushing furiously. Once she put her glass down, she said, "I'm just sorry I didn't kill that brother of mine. Would've saved me years of grief."

Blake's face darkened. "That's another one I'd rip from his balls to his brain if he was still alive."

"Shall we chat about something more appropriate for dinner?" Alice suggested. "There will be plenty of death talk here, and damned soon."

"Of course, love." Jed placed a hand over hers. "Dish up, everyone. Food's over on the sideboard in chafing dishes to keep things hot."

Sophie ate until she couldn't hold anymore. Between Blake, Gideon, and Mac, the men kept her plate full to overflowing. She'd never once gotten up to look at the buffet. Plates materialized in front of her, accompanied with comments suggesting she try the venison or the beef or the risotto.

"No more." She held up a hand. "Who made all this?"

"Mostly me," Megan said.

"Karl and I helped you, sweetheart," Les chimed in.

Megan broke into gales of laughter. "If you count sex on the kitchen table, sex up against the wall, and sex on the kitchen floor as help, then indeed, the two of you were stellar."

"We aim to please." Karl's dark eyes shone with love for his mate.

"Are you certain you don't want dessert?" Blake asked Sophie.

"Maybe later, but not now."

"Would you like to walk with us through the gardens?" Gideon suggested. "It's not terribly cold out."

When Sophie looked inside herself, she realized she'd love a walk outside. Nature was her playground, the air she drew her power from. "That would be wonderful. Just let me get my boots on."

"We were hoping you'd say yes—" Blake got to his feet "—so we retrieved your boots and stockings from your room. Hope that was all right."

"Sure. Where are they?"

"By one of the settees next to the front door," Mac replied.

Blake stood behind her chair, pulling it out of the way, while Mac and Gideon helped her up.

Sophie shook free of them. "Stop that. I'm scarcely an invalid."

"But we want to take care of you," Blake said.

"Find some other ways." The words were scarcely out before she could've kicked herself. The double meaning was unmistakable. "Not what I meant," she muttered around a tongue thick with embarrassment.

"Too late!" Mac jumped all over her faux pas. "We'll take you up on that—if you'll let us."

Answering was too complicated, so she headed for the front door and sat to put her boots on. When she stood, Blake wrapped a soft, black cloak around her. In response to the question in her eyes, he said, "Alice handed it to me on my way out of the dining room."

The words *dining room* drew her up short. "I should help Megan clear things up and do dishes. She got stuck with making that entire, delicious meal. She shouldn't have to do all the clean up too."

"She won't have to," Gideon said. "I heard them talking. Alice and her three mates volunteered for kitchen duty. I believe there just might be a chocolate cake cooling on the kitchen ledge. They were talking about making frosting for it—and licking it off..." His voice faded to nothing, and he hunched his shoulders in embarrassment. "Sorry," he muttered. "Shifters are pretty frank when it comes to talking about sex."

Sophie laughed. "Really? I never would've guessed."

Blake held the front door for her. Half bowing he said, "We'll be right behind you."

Somehow, she didn't doubt it for a moment. "Gosh." She walked through the open door and headed for one of the fragrant, herb gardens toward the back of the property. "Doors. Chairs. If you don't watch it, you'll spoil me beyond redemption."

"That's kind of the idea," Mac said.

The men arranged themselves with Blake on one side of her and Mac and Gideon on the other as they strolled through the soft blackness of a mild evening. Blake cleared his throat. "What did Alice and Megan tell you about the mate bond?"

Sophie slowed, thinking. "Quite a bit, really," she replied. "That was when they were trooping wolf shifters through here every day, hoping one of the family groups might be a match."

"Could you elaborate on what you know about the bond?" Gideon asked. "We want to make certain you have all the information you need to make a decision, but we don't want to bore you, either."

Sophie didn't think she'd ever get bored. She loved listening to all of them. Blake's voice was deep and musical, Gideon's a slightly higher baritone, and Mac's held a hint of an Irish twang with a lyrical cadence to his words. Arousal that had simmered since she'd driven home with the three men ratcheted up a notch, but she rode herd on it.

"If you'd rather not dredge up what the women told you," Mac cut in, "we can cover everything."

With a start, she realized she'd been lost in thinking about their voices—and their bodies. "Sorry. I'm kind of distracted."

"So are we," Blake murmured near her ear, sending shivers up and down her neck.

"What Alice and Megan said is the bond is for life. They said I'll live longer, but not as long as you, and that I'll get an infusion of magic through the bond. Megan seemed to think it would complement and strengthen my Indian power."

"Did the women mention how dangerous it is to link your star to ours?" Gideon asked. "Things are heating up. There may be a full out war soon. If that happens, the three of us might be gone for long periods of time leading our people against shifter enemies."

Sophie turned a corner, heading for a rose garden that seemed to bloom all year. "In case you missed it, being an Indian here in the U.S. hasn't exactly been a picnic. White men drove us from our lands and corralled us on reservations—crappy land no one else wanted for anything."

"At least they're not killing you outright," Blake broke in.

"Not anymore," she corrected. "And not directly. Now they just give us all the hooch we can drink, stand back, and let us self-destruct."

Gideon and Mac switched places so now Mac was right next to her. "One more important point," Mac murmured, "is once we make love, you won't ever be able to get us out of your mind or your heart. There's no leaving. No divorce. No out clause."

"I understand. The women said the same, but they also said they couldn't imagine leaving their mates."

Blake stopped walking and turned her to face him. "That's the mate bond. When you open yourself to it—to us—it will fulfill each of us, enrich our lives beyond measure." He tightened his grip on her upper arms. "I can't use magic to persuade you. It's against our covenant. If you want time to consider being our mate, we fully understand."

Mac and Gideon flanked Blake, so all three of them gazed at her. "We have no idea how tomorrow's meeting will go," Gideon said.

"If the will of the clans is to take a stand, to stop hiding who and what we are, coyote clan will stand with our brothers." Blake stood tall. "It also means we'll be leaving here, and I have no idea when we'll return. I already spoke with Jed, and he expects you'll remain with Alice and Megan."

Sophie thought about what there was to return to on the Big Pine reservation. Not very much. Here she had friends. People who understood her, and who cared about her.

"Those who care about you," Blake's deep voice rumbled, "include us."

"You were inside my head."

He nodded, those glittering, aquamarine eyes never leaving her face. "I want to know everything there is to know about you. So do Mac and Gideon. We're different from the wolf clan. Less bound by convention."

Sophie nodded slowly. She knew all about coyotes. Sly, skilled hunters who didn't mix with other species. Wolves formed bonds outside their own kind. Coyotes not so much. "How can you be sure I'm the right mate for you?"

"The mate bond never lies," Gideon said simply. "Many women have crossed our path over the long years we've been a family, but none of them sang to us like you."

"Hell," Mac cut in. "None of them sang to us at all. Not so much as a flicker."

She cocked her head to one side. "You've never had a mate."

"Never," Blake said and cupped the side of her face. "Will you be ours, Sophie? We'd love and care for you for the rest of your days. And the children you bear us too. The males will all be shifters. The girls would share your magic."

Desire winged through her, heating her blood. The men's words rang with sincerity, and all of them wanted her. She sensed their lust, but it was different from Abe's and the man she'd killed earlier. Where their desire had felt sick and twisted, what called to her tonight was pure, laced with longing and tenderness.

"Would you like us to leave you alone to think?" Blake let go of her and dropped his hands to his sides. The place where his hands had been felt empty, and she wanted him to touch her again.

"This morning." She ducked her head, finding it hard to meet their direct gazes.

"What about this morning?" Blake prodded.

"Alice and Megan hurried to the kitchen to get me. Guess everyone felt the mate bond magic explode. I didn't know what it was, so they had to tell me. It didn't take much talking before I was on my way to the small parlor to meet you. I was hopeful you'd be my mates. Living with everyone in this house convinced me of the beauty of the mate bond, and I've been disappointed every time a family group came to the house, and I didn't feel anything." She hesitated, unsure how much to share. "I started thinking there was something wrong with me. That what Abe did damaged me beyond salvation."

"Aw, sweetheart." Mac drew her against him, stroking her hair. The other men hugged her from both sides, murmuring.

"Definitely not damaged," Blake told her. "I already consider you our mate, whether or not you accept the bond."

The heat from their bodies surrounded her. Desire engulfed her, but it was mingled with apprehension. What if she wasn't good enough? What if she panicked during lovemaking and bolted from the bed?

"We'll go as slow as you need us to," Blake said, clearly having been in her thoughts.

"We want to please you," Gideon murmured. "We can take care of ourselves until you get comfortable with all three of us."

Sophie felt herself nodding against Mac's chest.

"Is that a yes?" Blake asked. "Do you want to join our family as our mate?"

Sophie pushed back enough to look at the three coyote shifters. "It is a yes." She smiled softly. "I'm not sure when I've wanted anything more."

Howls and yips split the night air. Even though the men still looked human, they sounded like the animals they were.

Footsteps pelted toward them as everyone came at a dead run. Alice and Megan pushed between Sophie and her mates. "We won't stay—" Alice shot a meaningful glance at Jed, Bron, and Terin "—but we had to congratulate you."

"It's not a done deal until they're mated," Jed reminded his mate with mock severity. He addressed his next words to Sophie. "I got to thinking about your Native magic, and realized it would blend far better with air than earth."

"What do you mean?" Sophie met his direct gaze.

"Each shifter clan has an affinity for one of the elements," Jed explained. "For wolves, it's earth. For coyotes, air."

"Mountain cats prefer fire, and bears water," Blake finished for Jed.

"Fascinating." Sophie smiled. "I want to hear more—not right now, but soon."

Les and Karl and Megan pumped everyone's hands. As quickly as they'd converged on the rose garden, the others melted into the shadowy night.

Blake held out a hand. So did the other men.

Sophie's heart beat too fast. Desire pummeled her from all sides.

"Take Blake's hand," Gideon urged. "He's our alpha. He'll lead you inside."

Feeling suddenly shy, she gripped Blake's proffered hand. Mac and Gideon walked behind her, each with a hand on one of her shoulders.

"You're taking me to way more than inside," she said. "You're leading me into a whole new life."

"For us too." Blake bent and kissed the side of her neck.

Sophie stopped, turned, and wove her arms around his neck. Blake didn't hesitate. He crushed his mouth atop hers. Mac and Gideon stung kisses down the sides of her face and stroked her arms and back. Now that she wasn't fighting the mate bond, it flamed hot, igniting her core with need for the men ringed around her. Lust spilled through her, and her magic blazed up brighter than ever before.

Suddenly she couldn't wait. Tearing her mouth from Blake's, she said, "Take me inside. Or we'll end up making love where we stand."

Blake scooped her up as if she weighed nothing and headed for the house at a dead run with his lieutenants flanking them.

CHAPTER 10

*D*esperate sexual hunger speared Blake, almost to the point of pain. He cradled Sophie against him, thanking every deity in the shifters' pantheon that his thoughtless words from earlier hadn't stolen the possibility of a mate away from him and his family group. Sophie felt good in his arms, all firm muscle and curves. She was tall for a woman, almost of a height with himself and his lieutenants.

When she'd entered the dining room with her hair swirling about her like a silver-splashed, dark cloud, he hadn't been able to stop staring. Her unbound hair lent her an ethereal aspect, like a goddess who'd graced their presence. Silver streaks framed her face and trailed down her back, nested in shiny black waves. Her hair was so long, it was possible she'd never cut it.

His cock throbbed where it pressed against the front of his trousers. Aroused ever since he'd opened his mind to the possibility of the mate bond, he'd denied himself release. Even though he'd been far from sure she'd accept them, he held back from bringing himself to orgasm. His mate deserved the best he had to offer.

Gideon tugged one of the side doors into Jed's mansion open, and Blake carried Sophie one flight up to the suite of rooms he and his lieutenants shared. While Sophie slept away what was left of the afternoon, they'd done their best to create a welcoming environment for her.

"Almost there, darling." He smiled at her.

"I could've walked." She grinned back.

"But then I wouldn't have had you this close to me." He snugged his grip, pulling her tighter against his chest.

This time, it was Mac who opened the door. "We hoped this would be all right," he told Sophie. "If you'd rather, we can visit one of the sunken tubs or the indoor pool on the lower level."

She squirmed in Blake's arms, and he set her down. "Oh my!" A hand flew to her chest. "It's lovely. Wherever did you get all these flowers?"

"Jed's garden and a local florist shop," Gideon answered, looking pleased.

"But all these roses and chrysanthemums must've cost a fortune," she protested.

"We've been alive for hundreds of years," Blake said. "Money isn't a problem—not for any shifter. We wanted something special just for you, and the flowers were Gideon's idea. Tell us how you'd like to begin, darling. Is this room all right? Would you like us one at a time? Or maybe just one of us tonight—"

She held up a hand. "How would you usually begin with a new mate?"

"Every family group finds their own way," Mac said, "but the bond isn't complete until each of us has consummated it. Sometimes that takes months or years if one of the men in a family group is away. Or the mate feels conflicted about bonding to more than one man."

"Is that common?" Sophie asked.

"Not really," Blake answered. "The mate bond always takes care of things like that. If you joined with one of us, eventually you'd find the others irresistible too."

Sophie nodded her understanding. "Maybe just let things begin and see where they take us?"

Blake looked solemn. "If you want us to stop at any time—no matter what's happening, all you have to do is tell us, and we will. You have control over how we come together."

"That's good, for someone like me."

"It's good for anyone," Gideon cut in. "No one deserves to have something happen to them that they're not one hundred percent in favor of."

"May we undress you?" Mac knelt by her feet and unlaced her boots. She balanced with a hand on his shoulder as he drew them off one at a time.

"How about if I undress you?" she countered.

"No complaints from me." Blake grinned. "Who do you want to start with?"

She sent a mischievous smile skidding his way. "It's a hard choice."

"No, we're hard." Gideon patted the front of his trousers. "Choices are easy since you'll end up with all three of us naked."

"Hopefully you too." Mac grinned boyishly.

Sophie walked to Blake and reached to unbutton his shirt. His heart hammered against his chest when she touched him, and it was all he could do not to crush her to him and start pulling her clothes off. She slid his shirt off his shoulders and draped it over a chair. Next, she ran gentle fingertips over his back and chest, walking around him as she looked at his body.

He itched to undo his belt and let his trousers fall to the floor, but he didn't want to push her or frighten her. Tonight had to unfold on her schedule, not his, Mac's or Gideon's. She was stroking his torso now with long, tentative strokes. He imagined what her hands would feel like wrapped around his cock and a low, feral moan tore from him.

Sophie stopped dead. "Did I hurt you?"

"No. It's just I want you so much, my throat couldn't contain it."

"I want you too." Her gaze scuttled away. "But I feel the same about Mac and Gideon." Color splotched her cheeks, and her breathing grew faster as she moved to Mac and tugged his sweater over his head. Next she unlaced the ties on Gideon's leather shirt and pulled it off his shoulders. When she straightened, her nipples showed through the fabric of her top.

"You're all beautiful, but in different ways." She moved among them, stroking and touching as waves of lust rolled through the room.

Blake toed off his shoes so they wouldn't tangle in his pants when she got around to removing them. He was so aroused, every cell quivered with anticipation. He wouldn't last long. None of them would, but among them, they'd see to her pleasure.

Sophie took hold of the bottom of her top and pulled it over her head. Next she unclasped her brassiere. "There," she said breathlessly. "We got the top half out of the way."

Blake couldn't take his eyes from her breasts. "You're beautiful," he ground out.

"You have the body of a goddess," Gideon panted, placing a hand over his crotch. "Sorry, I have to touch myself. It hurts not to."

"Sure and I've never seen finer breasts," Mac lapsed further into his Irish lilt, while rubbing his engorged flesh.

Blake's hand strayed toward his center, but he pulled it back.

Sophie's gaze moved from one to the other of them. She was frankly panting now. "Maybe that's as good a way to begin as any other," she said.

"What is?" Blake asked.

"I just discovered how to touch myself. I'd love to watch the three of you." Color suffused her face, turning her coppery skin a lovely rose.

"Are you going to finish undressing us first?" Gideon asked archly.

She glided in front of him and knelt, unlacing his shoes. Once he pushed out of them, she ran her hands up his legs eliciting a long groan from him, before undoing the fastenings of his pants. They slid down his legs and he stepped out of them. His cock stood out from his body, thick and hard.

Sophie moved to Blake next and unhooked his belt. Next came his trousers. Once they pooled in a heap at his feet, he kicked them aside. He'd never been quite this hard, and he was afraid if he so much as glanced at his cock, it would erupt spontaneously. When Sophie closed her hand around him, he was lost. He wanted her so much he couldn't bear not to touch her, so he ran his hands down her bare back, hoping he wouldn't spook her.

She leaned into his touch. "Nice. You feel amazing."

"Mac still has his pants on," Blake reminded her. It damn near killed him. He wanted to keep touching her—and have her keep touching him, but she'd crafted a plan for them, and by God, they'd stick to what she wanted.

"So he does." Sophie murmured, her full lips swollen with wanting all of them. Her nipples formed tight buds. Dark copper, they topped her lush breasts. Blake wanted to touch them, roll them between his fingers and watch her face as sensation poured through her.

She moved to Mac's side. His shoes were already off, and she undid his pants in record time. Both of them pushed the garment to the floor, and then Sophie spun away from him. Standing in the rough middle of a circle they formed around her, she unfastened her skirt, letting it fall to the floor. She hesitated for the space of two breaths before she pushed her underwear off her hips and stood naked before them.

"Jesus!" Blake almost couldn't breathe. Sculpted ribs led to a flat stomach and high, shapely hips. She had a well-formed ass and long, graceful legs. Dark curls, spiky with moisture, graced the vee between her legs.

"You're gorgeous," Gideon mangled the words, and Mac reverted to Gaelic, something he did when he was too overcome to cull through his brain for English.

Blake reached for his cock, but stopped. "Do you want us to touch ourselves now?" His voice cracked with the tension of holding himself back. The mate bond had him by the short hairs, and it wouldn't let up until he sank his cock inside their new mate. This first climax would be merely an appetizer, made all the more titillating because she'd be watching them.

SOPHIE'S THROAT WAS TIGHT. She wanted the men so much, it was all she could do not to throw herself onto the bed and open herself. Her clit throbbed, and her nipples were such stiff peaks they ached. She longed to wrap her hands and body and mouth around those three beautiful cocks. Blake's was thicker, nested in its mat of blond hair. Mat's was a bit longer, and Gideon's beautifully shaped. His skin was darker than the other two, and coal black hair curled around the base of his erect shaft.

She was so hot she couldn't talk, so she just nodded at Blake. He wrapped a hand around his cock and began pumping up and down his shaft. The others did the same. Their nipples formed peaks just like hers as they teased their engorged flesh. Because she couldn't stand not to, she sank a hand between her legs, rubbing hard.

"Yes," Blake panted, jacking himself harder. "Touch yourself. Make yourself come, sweetheart."

The men moved inward until all of them ended up close enough to touch her. Their cocks rubbed against her sides and belly as the men worked themselves. When Blake pushed a leg between hers, she welcomed the contact. The heat of his flesh against her clit, combined with her fingers, tumbled her over the edge and she came panting and bucking against him.

"Yes," Mac cried. "Now!" Semen pulsed from him in hot, white gouts.

"Right behind you," Gideon gasped as his cock jumped and shuddered.

Semen splashed her and the men rubbed it into her skin.

Blake made a wonderfully male sound just before his cock erupted, bathing her with still more jism. Because her gaze was glued to his hand and his cock, she saw he was still working himself, and his erection hadn't subsided. She wanted that cock. Wanted all the cocks inside her. She may have just come, but she needed more.

"It's the mate bond." Gideon ran a hand down her breast and twirled the nipple. "You'll just keep on wanting us."

"And us you," Mac murmured, capturing her other breast.

Blake slashed his mouth down on hers and thrust his tongue into her mouth. She sucked hungrily while all of them edged toward the bed. Blake stopped kissing her long enough to sit with his back against the wall, legs splayed, dead center on the bed. He ran a hand up his shaft and beckoned. "Come sit on me, darling."

She made her way up the bed and straddled him, letting his cock stretch her as he sank inside. Dear God, but he felt good. Mac moved in from one side, and Gideon the other, tweaking and pinching her nipples. She reached to both sides and held onto their cocks.

Blake groaned and thrust inside her, hands on her hips to set a rhythm. She moved up and down his shaft delighted as another peak built deep in her belly. When delight was about to spill from her, fingers probed between her ass cheeks. It felt good. So good, she pushed back against them.

"I'd like to try my cock there," Gideon whispered in her ear.

She rocked forward and turned so she could kiss Mac full on the mouth while Gideon slid an inch inside her anus. Blake jammed hard into her, his ridged flesh swelling even bigger and his breathing fast. Gideon moved farther inside, and she had hold of Mac's cock, while he pumped into her hand.

Rich sensation pummeled her from every direction. The cock in her pussy coupled with the one in her ass set off nerves she never imagined she had. Mac moved closer, improving the angle as she worked his cock, and getting him into position to rub her clit. The addition of his fingers rolling her nub between them shot her past delight. Climax roared from her. The men just kept plumbing her and rubbing her and she kept right on coming, one peak piled atop the next. Somewhere in the midst of ecstasy that wouldn't quit, she felt the men release inside her. First Gideon, then Blake shuddered within her body, bathing her with the heat of their fluids.

Mac uncurled her fingers from his cock. She looked at him. "Don't you want to come again?"

"Of course." He gifted her with a dazzling smile that lit his features from within. "But I'd rather it was inside that gorgeous body of yours. If you're sore or too tired, though, I can wait."

Blake moved his hands from her hips to her shoulders. "Your call, darling. Everything tonight is for you."

Sophie squirmed around the hardness still lodged within her.

Gideon slowly withdrew. "I'm off to wash up a bit." He bent and kissed her full on the mouth, teasing her with his tongue. "Want to be ready to go for the next round."

"Hey!" Blake called after Gideon's retreating back. "Sophie may not want a third go round tonight. This is all pretty new for her."

She levered herself off Blake's hardness and turned to Mac who looked hopeful and resigned at the same time. He stood next to the bed, so she rolled off it and stood next to him, putting her arms around him. He hugged her back and lowered his mouth over hers. Sophie lost herself in kissing his firm, demanding lips. When his hands ranged over her back, she gave herself up to heat roaring through her.

Mac broke away from her mouth. "What'll it be, darling? Up to you." He filled his hands with her breasts and twirled her nipples into even stiffer peaks.

Blake moved over so they'd have room to lay down. His eyes were on fire with lust, despite having come twice. He patted the bed invitingly.

"God help me, but I want you," she panted. "I don't see how I can still be this hot, but I want you inside me."

Mac scooped her up, laid her on the bed, and knelt between her legs. Spreading her knees wide, he lowered his head and trailed kisses down her belly before settling his mouth over the center of her sensation. Instead of touching her, he breathed on her, bathing her overwrought center with heat.

Sophie's hips bucked. She grabbed Mac's head and tried to jam herself against his mouth, but he held firm. To make matters worse, Blake fondled her breasts, and Gideon knelt so he could cover her mouth with his.

One tongue swipe from Mac almost made her come. Before she could move away from Gideon's mouth for long enough to demand a second one, Mac slid upward, positioning the head of his cock at her entrance. She wrapped her legs around his hips and pulled him inside.

A flurry of Gaelic endearments surrounded her as he began to move, slowly at first and then with mounting fervor. She slammed upward, wanting the contact against her clit. Blake let go of one of her breasts and moved a hand between her and Mac, rubbing her.

Sophie gave herself up to passion swirling thick about her. She slid from one peak to the next before Mac juddered inside her, head thrown back as he cried his heat and hunger to the world.

"It's done."

Sophie heard Blake's words as if they were a long way distant. She unglued her mouth from Gideon's and smiled as she imagined one of the Sirens might've. "You're wrong," she told the alpha. "We've barely begun."

Blake grinned back, hot and profanely beautiful, desire stamped in every nuance of his face and body. "Would our brand new mate enjoy a bath or a swim before the next round?"

"A swim. We can all be nude."

"I like the way you think." Gideon poked Mac in the ribs. "Get your cock out of our mate so we can walk downstairs to the pool."

Mac elbowed him back. "You wouldn't be in such a rush if it was your cock."

"Likely not."

Sophie began to laugh. For the first time since she was very young, she felt light, happy, buoyant. A small inner voice cautioned that the gods didn't approve of too much joy, but she shushed it. She'd deal with tomorrow when it came. Tonight was for her and her new mates. Nothing and no one had a right to intrude on their bliss.

CHAPTER 11

Blake rolled gently out of the tangle of bodies and made a grab for his watch. One in the afternoon. Past time for him and his lieutenants to be up and about. He still needed to talk with Jed before the others arrived. For a long moment, he gazed at Sophie cradled between Mac and Gideon. Love and a savage protectiveness blotted out the rest of the world. He wanted to take her and his lieutenants to a place far from the mess playing out before them, but it wasn't realistic.

Where would they go? The moon? Some far corner of Russia or Africa? He supposed they could live on a boat, moving from place to place, but he took his commitment to the coyote clan seriously. He couldn't abandon them. Especially not now when shifters were facing annihilation.

He wanted to let her sleep longer. They'd been up virtually the whole night making love in every conceivable position. Once kindled, Sophie's sexuality wove into theirs, creating seamless crescendos of release. No matter how many times he sank into the wonder of her body, it just created deeper longing.

She must've sensed his gaze on her because she opened her

eyes. "Time to get down to business, huh?" she said. "The other alphas will be here soon."

He nodded. "I'd rather take you back to our home outside Las Vegas and hole up for the next couple of years, but—"

"I understand." She spoke over him. "Could the three of you do one thing for me before you get caught up in whatever the rest of today brings?"

"Of course," Gideon said, not sounding the least bit sleepy.

"Just tell us," Mac chimed in.

"I want to see you in shifted form."

"We can do that," Blake said. "Inside the house. There's not time to drive into the desert where no one would see us, and shifting even in Jed's gated gardens isn't safe, especially in daylight."

"Inside is good enough for me." Sophie disentangled herself from Mac and Gideon. Crawling over Gideon, she got to her feet. "The animal part of your nature is key to who you are. I'm falling in love with all of you, so I want to meet your coyotes too."

Deeply pleased by her request—and her saying the word love—Blake reached for his animal form. The air flashed and shimmered before his molecules metamorphosed into four furry legs and his sleekly muscled coyote body.

Mac and Gideon were right behind him. It took a moment before the air cleared from so much expended power.

"You're almost the same colors you were as men," Sophie exclaimed. Walking among them, she stroked them, burying her fingers in their pelts. "I've never seen a black coyote before." She lingered over Gideon, who leaned into her touch, licking her fingers.

Probably not one as light as me, either, Blake said into her mind. To her credit, she didn't look even mildly rattled.

You're tawny and copper mixed together, she told him, also using telepathy. *My, talking like this is a whole lot easier than it used to be.*

Mac nosed her with his snout, and she caught his head between her hands, planting a kiss on the end of his nose. "I'll look forward to when we can run like this. Three coyotes and me." A shy look bloomed on her face. "I can howl at the moon. I've done it a time or two when sound just burst from me. The moon has a pull. A strong one. It augments my power. Jed was partially right because I draw my magic from both earth and air."

"The moon enhances our ability too," Blake informed her. Summoning the transformation, he shifted back and drew her tight against him. "We have to clean up and meet with Jed."

"I should help the women—or Megan anyway," Sophie said. "Alice is wonderful, but the kitchen isn't her natural environment."

"Depending on when the others show up," Gideon said sounding hopeful, "maybe we might catch another hour or two together."

"I'll look forward to it." Sophie smiled shyly, as if she were trying out being happy. "No easy way to say goodbye, so I'm going to head for my room and take a quick shower."

She moved out of Blake's embrace and into first Mac's, then Gideon's, arms before wrapping a robe around herself and gliding out the door. Joy eddied around her. Blake wanted to capture the moment, make it last forever. Instead, he turned to his lieutenants.

"Back in battle mode, boys. Fast clean up, then we're going to hunt Jed down."

"You got it." Gideon loped toward the bathroom.

"We finally have a mate." Mac beamed. "Now let's make certain we create a world where she can walk proud by our side."

"It's one of the things I want to hammer out with Jed. Let's get moving." Blake clapped his lieutenant on the shoulder and together they walked toward the sound of water splashing in the bathroom.

~

Jed, Bron, Terin, Les, and Karl hunched around the radio, listening intently. At the sound of the study door opening, Jed turned. Seeing Blake and his men, he motioned them to silence and made room in the circle around the radio.

"...two distinct camps are emerging in Washington," the announcer droned on. "Part of Congress wants to focus on the upcoming conflagration in Europe because Germany never did give up, despite losing the last war. A different segment of our leadership is busy ignoring Europe while they draft plans to clear the scourge of shifters off American soil."

"Do you have an opinion?" the news co-anchor asked.

"Funny you should ask. I do, but of course it's not for the public airwaves." The announcer laughed, but it sounded canned. "This is Skylar signing off for KMVR. Tune in tomorrow same time, same station, for the best of, the top of, the nation's news."

Bron flipped off the set and turned his attention to Jed. "What do you make of that, boss?"

Jed narrowed his eyes. "The part about not everyone in DC being after us shocks me, but it has to be a good thing. Could one of you run out and get an LA Times?"

"I'll go." Terin bolted for the door. "Back soon."

"While we're waiting for him to get back," Jed said, turning toward Blake. "Congratulations. I'm happy for you."

"Thank you." Blake extended a hand and Jed shook it, followed by Gideon's and Mac's. "You understand why we'll forego a ceremonial celebration."

"Maybe we could take a raincheck," Gideon said.

"Yes, after our victory," Mac added.

"You hope there's a victory." Blake shook his hair over his shoulders. "Just because not everyone in DC is out for our hides, doesn't mean things will get much easier."

"We have to prevail," Mac said simply. "We have a mate to protect and watch over."

"We know exactly how you feel," Karl said. "Megan means everything to us."

"Moving beyond our mates, even though it's difficult, the first part of the broadcast detailed what happened in the Palisades," Jed cut in. "Thank all the gods who watch over us, no one knows what happened to that passel of Hunters."

"Did they identify them as Hunters?" Blake asked.

"Not in so many words," Jed replied. "No one's supposed to know they exist. Part of their vows include secrecy." He exhaled sharply. "Hell, these are modern times. The existence of a secret hit squad, whose raison d'être was to murder shifters, wouldn't be well received, no matter how much people fear us."

"Right you are, boss," Bron said. "They're good with us rotting in jail until we die. It's much more humane than killing us outright. Without due process."

"What exactly did the broadcast say?" Blake persisted.

"That seventy-four men entered the Sierra at the Glacier Lodge portal and disappeared without a trace. Rangers are still combing the mountains with search dogs, but they're coming up dry."

"We'll have to let Keir know he outdid himself." Blake chuckled grimly. "He did tell me that the animal scents from all of us would confuse the hell out of bloodhounds. Turns out he wasn't just blowing smoke."

"Regardless." Jed rolled his eyes. "We escaped a speeding bullet."

"Do you think it would help if we went to Washington with Keir and Jon?" Blake met Jed's gaze. "Plead our cause with words rather than our fangs and claws?"

Jed drew his brows together into a thick, worried line. "Risky. We'd have to reveal what we are. We can't just show up and say we represent friends who are shifters. Fraternization is almost as big a sin as being one. Plus sending all four alphas into the lion's den isn't wise."

Terin blew back through the door, a thick tube of newsprint rolled under one arm. "I got several," he announced. "That way we can all read it. Shit! The Palisades made the front page."

Blake took one of the papers and retired to a corner with his lieutenants. Jed did the same with Bron and Terin. Les and Karl took the third paper, moving under a window where the light was better. For a time, the only sounds in the room were the rattle of paper and an occasional burst of cursing.

"Great photo of Lon Chaney's cabin," Les said.

"Be grateful it's a mug shot of wood and fieldstones and not us," Jed muttered. "At least we didn't make the hit parade of the reporter's speculations about what happened to the Hunters."

"Reporter was pretty sharp, though," Bron said.

"I thought so too," Blake replied. "What particular part were you focused on?"

"Right here." Bron pointed. "Where he mentioned how odd it was that none of the men had any immediate family. No wives. No girlfriends. Scarcely even a parent or aunt or uncle to be found."

"Bet the gang at Hunter Central are seething," Les said.

"We don't know there's any such thing," Jed cautioned.

"There has to be," Les replied. "They have to get their orders from somewhere. If the Church doesn't still oversee the operation, it has to be an elite group of Hunters."

"You may be onto something," Blake said.

"Huh?" Jed turned toward him. "What?"

"If there's some sort of central command structure, and I'm with Les, there damn near has to be. How about if we target them? Do a stealth operation and wipe them out. It might demoralize the rest of them enough, they'd fade into obscurity—at least for a while."

Jed's canines lengthened. His wolf loved the idea. "It's a possibility. Let's wait until Keir and Jon get here, and we'll run it up the flagpole."

"We could do both things," Gideon spoke quietly. "Go to Washington and wipe out the group in charge of Hunters."

"Heard my name." Keir pushed through the door with Jon right behind him.

"Did those discerning Ursidae ears hear anything else?" Jed smiled. He'd always liked the big, swarthy shifter.

"Some. Let's wait until our boys get here. They're parking the cars." He eyed Jed. "Your driveway's big, but it's getting crowded down there."

"With all due respect—" Jed swept his gaze over the cozy study's inhabitants "—it's hard enough for four to come to consensus. How about if our lieutenants spent the next hour elsewhere?"

"I'm good with that." Bron punched Terin lightly in the arm. "Let's go entertain our mate."

"Aw geez. Really?" Jed stomped over to the large fireplace that took up most of one wall. "I'll be here sweating bullets to decide the safest route for our people, and you'll be keeping our mate company."

"Damn straight." Terin followed Bron out of the room. "It's a tough job, but—"

"Go. Give Alice my best." Jed chopped the air dismissively with one hand. He'd much rather be cuddling with their mate than crafting war strategy, but that was scarcely something he could give voice to. Or even think too loudly.

Les and Karl left next.

"You sure you won't need us?" Gideon asked Blake.

"If I do, you won't be far. I liked Bron's idea. Why don't you find Sophie? Bet she's worried about us."

"We don't have our mate anywhere close—" the bear lieutenants, Waldo and Brune, poked their heads through the study door "—but we get the picture. Call us when you need us. We'll be in the kitchen eating our way through Jed's larder."

"Us too," the mountain cat lieutenants said and trotted down the hall.

"Shit! Double jeopardy. My lieutenants are with our mate, and we'll be lucky if there's so much as a cracker left once your boys get done." Jed shook himself from stem to stern. "Let's get down to it. Did you either read or hear the news?" he asked Keir and Jon.

"Yup." Keir nodded. "Regular mixed bag."

"It could be worse," Jon said. "They could've figured out what really happened to all those Hunters."

"Not on my watch." Keir curled his upper lip. "For anyone to figure things out, they'd have to know a hell of a lot more about Hunters than they currently do. No one outside their ranks knows they track us to kill us."

"And they can't exactly run to the authorities and tell them they deployed a large Hunting party to string us up," Blake said. "It would break their whole secrecy deal."

"Do we have any idea how many of those bastards actually exist?" Jon asked.

Jed shook his head. "Unless we discovered where their headquarters is and broke in, we'd never get hold of that kind of information."

"Even if we did," Keir pointed out, "they could've written everything in code."

"Gideon is pretty good at deciphering that kind of thing," Blake said. "It's moot, though, since we have no idea where they're located."

Jed perched on the back of one of the large, leather couches lining the study and folded his arms across his chest. "We were listening to a radio broadcast before you got here," he said to Keir and Jon.

"And?" Keir made come along motions with one hand.

"Apparently we have at least a few friends in DC who want to call off the witch hunt. Or at least their preference is to focus on the escalating political tension in Germany."

Jon broke into a broad smile. "Really? That's excellent news."

Keir frowned, creating a mass of furrows across his broad forehead. "It's because Congress is worried about another war in Europe, and they don't want to split their focus."

"True," Jed said. "But does the why of things really matter?"

"Tell me what you're thinking," Keir prodded. "I know that look on your face, and it rarely bodes well."

Jed nodded once, sharply. "We need to locate the Hunters' primary headquarters. Once we've done that, we can steal their records—"

"—and hunt down every one of those sons of bitches," Jon cut in.

"After we kill their leaders," Jed said.

"It's possible once no one is left to issue orders, their whole operation will fall apart," Blake said thoughtfully. "And if it didn't, once we knew who they were, they could begin to disappear. Quietly. Dead of night sort of thing."

"What do you want to do about Congress?" Jed asked.

"Why don't we let them hash shit out while we take care of the Hunters?" Keir suggested. "We can decide about them once we finish what's far more immediate and important." He paused to take a measured breath. "The best thing about the Palisades was how good it felt to kill those fuckers."

"Yeah!" Jon jumped in with both feet. "We got to kill in animal form and destroy those abominations. I'm sorry we didn't do it years ago."

"In truth, so am I," Jed said. "I kept hoping if we laid low, a peaceful solution would rise to the top. Except one never did."

"So. It appears our first order of business is figuring out where the Hunters have their headquarters," Keir muttered. "Once we know how well-guarded it is, we can launch enough men to take it down."

"It's possible our new mate might be able to help," Blake said.

Jed slitted his eyes. "How so? We determined she had no ties to that brother of hers."

"Indeed, but she saw him in visions. Maybe some of those revealed his location." Blake shrugged. "I hate to even ask because her brother is such a sore subject, but it seems to me she's our best potential lead at the moment."

"He has a point," Jon said. "It could take us months of searching, and we might not find them. Too bad none of us looked at the registration certificates inside their cars or jotted down all those license plates from the trail parking lot in the Palisades, but we were in such a godawful hurry to get out of there, I didn't even think about it."

"Wouldn't have bought us much," Keir said. "We killed all of them. Don't need to know where they live—or their names."

Jed got to his feet and trotted over to where one of the LA Times lay spread across an oak table. After rustling through a few pages, he said, "This is better than license plates. There's a list of the missing men's names in the Times. Thought I saw it earlier."

"Maybe I'm overlooking something—" Jon set his mouth in a hard line "—but how is knowing where the Hunters lived going to tell us squat? Unless some of them lived at their headquarters."

"I still think Sophie is our best bet," Blake said. "Once we're done here, I'll go ask her."

"It's not like her visions yield addresses," Keir grumbled.

"No, but they might have landmarks one of us recognizes," Blake persisted.

Jed walked to where Keir stood and faced him. "What's bothering you? Spit it out now."

"The woman. I wanted her dead, but you insisted on showing mercy."

Blake was on his feet in an instant. He lunged in front of Keir. "She's my mate," he hissed. "You'll keep a civil tongue in your head."

Keir growled.

Blake snarled back.

Jed stepped between them and put a hand on each man's chest, pushing them away from one another. "For Christ fucking sakes, stop it." He looked hard at Keir. "You wanted her dead because you were afraid she'd reveal what she knew. Well, she's mated to one of us now, so she's caught up in the magic of the mate bond. She'd die before she'd see anything bad happen to her mates, and you know it."

"You had no idea that would happen." Keir scowled.

"Of course I didn't," Jed agreed. "But it is one less problem, and she's made three of our own very happy. Can you let this drop?"

After a long, low, rumbling growl, Keir nodded. He extended a hand in Blake's direction. "Sorry, brother. It won't happen again."

Blake took the bear clan alpha's hand, and Jed blew out a relieved breath. They had far bigger problems than Keir's control issues. The bear shifter had wanted something specific to happen. When it didn't, he'd done a slow burn. Jed was grateful Sophie was mated. If she was just sitting with the other women or up in her room, he wouldn't have put it past Keir to see she met with an untimely accident—or just disappeared.

"So," he said briskly. "We have the beginnings of a plan. Blake. Go talk with Sophie. If she has vision material that might help, bring her in here."

"Why?" Blake may have shaken Keir's hand, but he sounded sullen.

"Because one of us may recognize something in one of her visions that will lead us right to that vipers' nest of Hunter scum," Jed replied.

"I am sorry," Keir said. "I promise to treat her with the respect befitting the mate of an alpha."

"Appreciate it." Blake skewered the bear shifter with his unusual eyes. "I love her, and I'd fight anyone to the death who so much as looked askance at her."

"I get that." Keir laughed. "I'm newly mated myself."

Jed sent a meaningful look Blake's way to get him moving. The coyote shifter nodded his understanding just before he strode briskly from the room.

CHAPTER 12

Earlier that day

Sophie made her way to the kitchen after she left her mates. It was moving on toward the middle of the afternoon, but she wanted to help Alice and Megan if she could. Soon the house would be full of men with big appetites, which meant lots of food preparation. She was a credible cook, and if she could spell Megan, she would.

She floated through a shower and combing out her damp hair. Her body still tingled from her lovers' touches and kisses. Deeply happy, thoroughly satiated, she pictured the men in her mind's eye while she dressed. Each was exquisitely beautiful, with slabs of muscle running the length and breadth of their bodies. She'd touched and sucked and kissed every inch of all of them, and then done it again. When she tried to capture her favorite parts of their lovemaking, she couldn't settle on any one thing. She'd adored all of it. They'd worshipped her body and made her feel special, loved, cherished.

She hoped she'd returned their adulation in kind. They'd bent a whole lot of their preconceived notions to accept her into their family group. Especially Blake. He'd apologized over and over until she laid a hand over his mouth and told him all was forgiven.

She was about to head downstairs when knocking sounded on her door, just before Megan and Alice pushed it open. Both women sported Cheshire cat grins, and Alice kicked the door shut behind them.

"Tell us." She plopped down on the bed.

"Yes," Megan seconded. "Everything. Oooh, look. Sophie's blushing."

"We understand," Alice said. "Because it's something we live every day. Sex with shifter mates is the greatest gift a woman can imagine—and then some. They're wonderfully attentive."

"And they can see into your mind," Megan spoke up. "So they know exactly what you need. After Les and Karl and I got some miles under our belts, I could do the same thing. We've even shared our magic, so I sensed how their bodies felt inside me. It was pretty damned amazing, let me tell you. I'd always wondered what sex felt like to a man. Well, now I know."

Sophie swallowed hard. She'd never talked openly about sex with anyone before. Since it seemed like safer ground, she retreated to magic. "Tell me more about the power you absorbed from your mates. Do you think it will enhance what I already have from my Indian blood?"

"Oh my, yes!" Megan's blue eyes shone with warmth. "I was stuck in jail in Red Deer—that's a little town in Alberta—and this amazingly powerful medicine woman rescued me. When I asked how she came to be so strong magically, she told me it was because she was married to shifters."

"Both of us can communicate with our minds now," Alice said. "According to Jed, my abilities will continue to develop over the next few years. Pregnancy should enhance them even more."

"Are you planning to have a baby right away?" Sophie asked.

Alice shook her head. "Jed's worried about if we'll even be able to stay here. He wants to make certain we have a stable household before we add to it."

"Shifters control when we get pregnant," Megan told her. "So it's not something we have to even think about."

Sophie's face heated. Babies had been the last thing on her mind the previous night. When she'd belatedly thought maybe they should've used condoms, so much semen had flowed into her, she decided to let the chips fall where they would.

"I was on my way downstairs when you showed up," she said hurriedly, fearing the conversation would revert back to sex. "Can I help with food or anything before all those extra men show up here?"

It was Megan's turn to blush. "I, erm, ordered a bunch of stuff from a catering company. It should show up soon. Don't tell the guys."

"Your secret's safe with me." Sophie grinned. "Did you order everything, or is there still something to do in the kitchen?"

"Plenty to do," Alice said. "We only ordered a roast beef and two chickens. And desserts." She scrunched her nose at Sophie. "You never did give us any juicy details about last night."

"And I'm not going to. Not yet anyway." Sophie chewed her lower lip. "What happened between the men and me felt sacred. Talking about it doesn't seem right, somehow."

"I understand." Megan moved to her side and hugged her. "Alice and I were just so excited you accepted the mate bond, we wanted to hear all about it."

"Kitchen?" Sophie started for the bedroom door and opened it.

"If we have to." Alice lowered her voice conspiratorially. "You'll have guessed it's not my favorite place. I did spend some time looking over your balcony though. Climbing's a hobby of mine, so I duplicated what I figured you did, which was making your way to that big pine tree and thence to the ground."

"How'd it go?" Sophie turned to face Alice.

The other woman tossed her hands palms up. "Not bad. A few

dicey moments when that one ledge ran out above. I sort of dove for the tree."

Sophie snorted. "Yeah. Same thing I did."

With her friends flanking her, she made her way down two floors to the spacious kitchen. It was a cook's dream with shiny appliances and an endless supply of pots and pans. "I'll start on some fresh bread," she said.

Megan rubbed her hands together. "Excellent. I'll put on a big pot of potatoes to boil and cut up vegetables to cook."

"I'd just be underfoot," Alice announced and tugged out a kitchen chair. Turning it, she straddled the seat and draped her arms over the back.

"You could pour us some wine," Megan suggested.

Alice laughed. "Now that I can handle. Any preferences since I'm heading to the wine cellar?"

"Doesn't matter." Sophie shrugged. "When I drink at all, it's usually whiskey, but booze isn't good for Indians. We can't break it down."

Alice returned with two bottles of Cabernet and a bottle of Chardonnay. Once she'd poured glasses for everyone, she sat back down. "I'm worried about the men," she said flatly. "They never exactly told us what happened up in the Palisades, only that they killed a number of Hunters."

"I've been keeping an ear on the news," Megan looked up from peeling potatoes and dropping them in a huge kettle of boiling water. "So far the whole thing is one big mystery. Kind of like the Lindbergh baby kidnapping."

"You know the whole story." Alice fixed her green gaze on Sophie, but she shook her head.

"That's for your mates to tell you. Besides, it was pretty ugly. I'd rather not relive it."

"We understand." Megan shot a reproachful look Alice's way.

"The guys are hatching something up," Alice muttered. "I know they are. If something happened to any of my mates, I don't know what I'd do. Go on a killing spree, maybe, and make certain whoever hurt them got what they deserved."

The kitchen door opened with a *swoosh,* and Blake strode in. "Hello, love." He walked behind Sophie and put his hands on both sides of her waist.

"Watch it," she cautioned. "I'm elbow deep in flour."

"You need to rinse off and come with me."

Sophie crossed the kitchen to the sink and splashed water on her dusty hands and arms. "Why?"

"We need information about Hunters. I'm hoping some of those visions where you saw your brother might yield clues about a location for them."

Sophie nodded and closed her teeth over her lower lip. "Maybe. I saw him plenty of times." She motioned to her bowl of half kneaded dough. "Could one of you finish that up and throw a tea towel over it?"

Alice sprang to her feet. "Sure. I may not enjoy cooking, but I'm a decent enough breadmaker."

"We'll help." Bron and Terin trooped into the kitchen, followed by Les, Karl, and the lieutenants for the other three clans.

Gideon and Mac hugged Sophie, passing her awkwardly between them while she hung a dishtowel over a rack. "We gave the guys a tour of the neighborhood," Mac said, "otherwise we'd have been here sooner."

"Anything we can eat right now?" Les asked, looking around hopefully.

The front doorbell chimed.

"The answer to that is probably yes." Megan grinned at her mate. "Want to answer that? I wasn't going to tell you I cheated, but it should be a man bearing food."

"You ordered food, rather than making it?" one of the men asked, his words dripping with censure.

Sophie gazed at him, taking his measure. She would've bet

money he was a bear shifter. Something about his burly build and the feel of his magic tipped her off.

"Yeah." Megan settled her hands on her hips and swung to face him. "You got a problem with that?"

The bear shifter looked away from her direct gaze. "No, ma'am."

"That's better." Les passed the other lieutenant on his way to the front door.

"We don't let anyone criticize our mate." Karl stalked to the bear shifter.

"Didn't mean anything by it," the man muttered. "Back off, brother."

"Come on." Blake hooked a hand through Sophie's bent elbow. "The other alphas are waiting."

She followed him out the door and into the study, sifting through her memories. "It might be easier," she murmured, "if I went into a trance state. Then you could pick through my—"

"Summon a trance if it helps, but then you'll have to tell us what you see. Culling through someone's mind is like hunting for a needle in a hayrick."

"Good news," Blake called to Jed. "The men just now made it to the kitchen, which means there might be something left to eat after we're done."

"Fat chance." Jed trotted to Sophie's side. "That's Keir, alpha for bears." He pointed. "The other man is Jon, alpha for mountain cats." Does the fact you're here mean you have information?"

"I'm not sure. I was just telling Blake I need to summon a trance. It will make it easier for me to recall my visions about Abe."

"What do you need to accomplish that?" Jed focused his direct gaze on her.

"Outside. Nature strengthens my abilities."

Blake shucked his sweater and wrapped it around her. Jed opened a glass door leading outside. "Easier than jumping, huh?"

She smothered a laugh. "Way easier, but Alice told me she duplicated my escape route handily."

"She what?" Jed drew back. "Christ! She never told me she went off your balcony like a goddamned cat burglar."

"Oops." Sophie made her way outside. "Guess I should've kept my mouth shut, but your mate is a mountain climber."

"As if I needed a reminder," Jed groused.

Sophie headed for the herb garden, drawing the sweater closer about her for warmth. Blake, Jed, Keir, and Jon followed. She picked a large, flat rock in the midst of basil and rosemary plants and settled into a cross-legged sit. The men, clearly no strangers to power, stayed well back.

She met Blake's wonderful eyes and he gazed at her, his features brimming with adoration and caring. "I'm going to hum to bring my energies in line with mother earth," she told the men. "As visions come to me, I'll describe what I see."

"How do we call you back?" Blake asked.

"Say my name into my mind, or just let the visions run their course."

Sophie shut her eyes and straightened her back. She didn't want to think about Abe, didn't want him in her mind at all. He made her feel dirty, used, but this was important. If she harbored clues about the Hunters' whereabouts, maybe it would help her mates and all the other shifters too.

The hum began deep in her chest and vibrated through her vocal chords. Slowly at first, then more quickly, visions of Abe filled her head. She let words flow as one sending morphed into another. Not exactly hearing her own voice, she transformed into a medium transmitting information from the spirit world to this one.

Time slithered past. She was aware of being cold, but not cold enough for it to matter. Her fingers tapped a rhythm to match her chant and hold her in trance. Darkness was falling when she heard Blake call her.

"Sophie. We have what we need. Sophie, darling, come back to me."

She struggled to open her eyes. They felt as if they'd been sealed shut. "How long?" she croaked around a throat dry as ground glass.

"Long enough, I was ready to call the game." Blake's tone was grim, and he drew her into his arms. His body felt wonderfully warm against her as he helped her stand.

"What did you learn from me?" She glanced from one man to the next.

"We identified three distinct locations," Jed ground out. "One of them isn't far from here. Just up in the San Gabriels."

"Where are the others?" When the men hesitated, she pulled away from Blake. "I have a right to know since the information came from me."

"Flagstaff, Arizona," Blake said. "And the northern Nevada desert outside Winnemucca. Let me get you inside, sweetheart. You're chilled clear through."

"Once you have your mate settled," Jed said, "return to the study so we can map out a plan."

Sophie leaned heavily against Blake. She felt weak, drained, as if she'd been awake for days.

"It's because you channeled so much magic," Blake said near her ear. He guided her upstairs to her room and started a hot bath running. "I can't stay, sweetheart, but you soak in that tub until you stop shivering. Then get yourself downstairs and sip a little whiskey. Probably by then, we'll all be in the kitchen or dining room. You need food to go along with the spirits."

She melted against him. "Yes, Daddy." Sadness filled her. "Too bad I never could say anything like that to my real dad."

Blake stroked her hair. "I love you, Sophie. You did us a great favor today. I hope it wasn't too upsetting."

"Not after the first few visions," she said and let him help her out of her clothes and into the steaming tub.

Desire for him heated her blood, but he turned to leave after a lingering kiss full of promise and hunger. "Later." He smiled knowingly. "I'll make up for leaving you alone once we've all eaten. So will Gid and Mac."

She sank into the deep tub, letting the water cover her shoulders. Even with the residue of Blake's love for her drifting in the steamy air, it took a long time before the chill left her bones.

An idea took root as she lounged in the water. At first it scared her so much, she chased it from her mind, but it kept returning. She could dream the future. Why not use her gift to find out how her mates would fare in the coming days? If a path they'd chosen led to disaster and they knew ahead of time, they could pick something different.

What if I find out one of them is going to die?

Her heart shriveled in her chest, and she curled into a tight ball under the water.

All I see are probabilities, she reminded herself. *If something I gin up can help them, I owe it to them to at least look.*

BLAKE RACED BACK to the study. Gratitude his mate was safe hastened his steps. More than anything, he wanted to get to the end of this mess so he could return home with Sophie and his lieutenants, preferably in a world where shifters could walk free.

"What's the plan?" he asked without preamble.

"How's your mate?" Jed countered.

"She's all right. Thanks for asking. Now what'd the three of you hatch up?"

"Something that makes sense," Jon spoke up. "We'll start with the nearest location and see what we find. If we get lucky, we'll hit the mother lode and not have to go any farther."

"But we need to wipe all of them out," Blake protested.

"Correct me if I didn't get this right," Jed said, "but my understanding was that Abe was a Hunter for the last eleven years.

Sophie was in trance for long enough to give us details spanning much of that timeframe. What if the Hunters moved their headquarters periodically?"

"They probably did. Maintaining more than a single primary location at any given time seems remote," Keir cut in.

"So we'll only need to keep looking until one of the locations looks inhabited," Jon clarified.

"Understood. When do we leave for the San Gabriel Mountains?" Blake asked. "How many will take part in the operation?"

A muscle danced in Jed's jaws as he clenched them together. "Whoa. Slow down. It's not like the Palisades. The San Gabriels are settled to some extent, which means we can't show up with several hundred of us without arousing extreme suspicion."

"So we send a few of us to scope things out," Blake said. "Once we know more, we can call for reinforcements. If they're close, telepathy would do the trick."

"Except Hunters would sense it," Keir said sourly.

"Maybe not," Jed spoke slowly. "There are enough radio towers up there, it might interfere with their ability to intercept our magic."

"I have another idea." Jon narrowed his eyes to slits. "It'll save time too."

"Spill it." Jed gestured with one hand.

"You and coyote clan can check out the San Gabriels. I'll take some of my boys and go to Flagstaff. Keir and his bears can take Winnemucca. That way, we'll know everything there is to know in just a few days."

Jed clasped his hands behind him and paced up and down the room, clearly weighing Jon's suggestion.

Blake liked it, but he kept his mouth shut. There were enough of them that splitting forces made a whole lot of sense. If they found a beehive of the bastards, they could strategize how best to take them down. However they proceeded, they'd have to strike fast and hard.

Jed looked up. "It's a sound idea. We'll leave early tomorrow."

Blake stepped in front of him. "So it's going to be you and your lieutenants plus me and mine?"

Jed frowned. "It's going to be damned difficult to tell Les and Karl they can't come."

"That's only eight of us. Not so bad in terms of drawing unwanted attention," Blake said. He liked the Canadian wolf shifters. They'd proven strong fighters in the last battle.

"We'll gather everyone for a brief meeting right after supper." Jed nodded sharply. "We'll have to determine who our leader and co-leader are."

"That's easy." Blake clapped him across the shoulders. "I won't fight you for the primary command position. I'm good with being second."

"Will your men agree?" Jed shot a penetrating glance his way.

"If I tell them that's how it is, of course they will. How about seeing after our mates and getting a spot of something warm to eat along with some stiff spirits?"

"Good idea." Jed walked out of the study with the others behind him.

Blake smiled inwardly at Jed's question about command structure. Coyotes weren't nearly as argumentative as wolves, but he kept that opinion to himself. It felt empowering to finally be taking matters into their own hands. Soon they'd shake off the yoke of human oppression. He was certain of it.

Deep within, his coyote howled with bitter laughter, and Blake choked back a snort. In addition to following orders better than wolves, coyotes were also a damn sight more arrogant, and he'd do well to keep it in mind. Gideon and Mac would follow his direction, but if Jed ordered them to do something they disagreed with, all bets were off.

CHAPTER 13

*D*inner had been a boisterous affair with many toasts for the newly mated family groups. Cognizant that the next day would start early for the men, no one lingered over their meal. Sophie, Alice, and Megan cleaned up while the men fine-tuned plans for the following day. Because three of them washed and dried, they were done in record time. It helped that all of them were anxious for some private moments with their mates. Sophie shared a quick hug with her friends.

"It'll be all right," she told them.

"How can you know?" Alice demanded, her eyes pinched with worry.

"I feel it." Sophie shrugged off a deeper answer. She didn't plan to tell the women about her scheme to call upon her gift to help the men. In case what she saw was unpleasant, she didn't want to see fear creep into the other women's eyes as they waited for their men to return.

"I sure as hell hope you're right," Megan murmured.

Sophie hoped so too.

"We're done in the kitchen." She bounded into the dining room and stood between Blake and Gideon.

"Probably as good a time as any to call it a night." Jed glanced at Alice. "None of us will be worth much, knowing our mates are waiting."

"Good call." Blake rose to his feet, followed by the rest of the men.

Demanding and full of promise, Sophie's mates' energy followed her up the stairs. Desire ran through her like a hot, viscous river. Getting down and intimate with her men was about to happen, and she couldn't wait for them to surround her with their love, heat, and need. Before they got to the door to their room, she turned to face Blake, Gideon, and Mac. "I want you more than life itself, but we have to stop after one round."

"Why, darling?" Blake threaded an arm around her waist and nuzzled her neck. "Are you sore from last night?"

"Of course I am, but that's not it." She pulled away so she could think more clearly. "I have the gift of farseeing. Don't you want me to look into the future and see what the San Gabriels hold for you?"

Jed drew his brows together. "Yes, and no. If you see danger, we'll likely go anyway."

"Depends on the danger, boss," Gideon pointed out. "They might be laying for us. It would be good if we had more information, so we were better prepared for what's out there."

"Are you sure you have enough energy after all the power you expended today for the alphas?" Mac stroked her arm, his eyes glowing with concern.

"I have plenty of juice left to call another trance. Once summoned, they just happen. The only power expenditure is at the beginning." She looked from one man to the next, almost undone by emotion sluicing through her. If anything happened to any of them, she'd be devastated.

"We accept your gift." Blake's tone was formal. "Now that's decided, let's forget about Hunters and tomorrow. Right now, there's just us and you, our mate."

"Agreed." Sophie spun and ran lightly through the open door leading into their room.

The men surrounded her, tag teaming removing her clothing. Mac knelt and unlaced her boots while Blake divested her of sweater and blouse. As soon as he unhooked her brassiere, Gideon filled his hands with her breasts and bent to suckle her nipples.

Heat pooled between her legs, sharp and urgent. Her shyness from the previous night completely gone, Sophie yanked at whatever parts of the men's clothing she could reach. When someone's fingers undid the buttons holding her skirt on her hips, it slid to the floor.

"I'm mostly naked." Breath thickened in her throat as desire overwhelmed her.

"You heard our mate." Blake's voice was harsh with wanting her. "I'm going to kiss her thoroughly. You two get those clothes off."

"Aw, I want to kiss Sophie," Mac teased, busy getting out of his boots.

Blake blotted out the rest of the world when he lowered his mouth and covered hers, probing for entrance with his tongue. She opened to him and sucked hungrily. Last night, she'd taken his cock into her mouth. It was the first time she'd ever done something like that, and she'd loved it.

The cock in question pressed against her belly, hot and hard and quivering with the same craving that made every one of her nerve endings tingle with white hot need. Blake cradled her head in his hands and licked, nipped, and sucked on her lips and tongue. She kissed him back with a desperation to match his own. Though only scant hours had passed since she'd left the men, lust seared her.

Gideon wrapped his arms around her from one side, and Mac from the other. They pushed her panties down her legs and rained kisses on her as they explored her breasts and belly. Someone reached between her legs from behind and began rubbing the center of her pleasure. Between his firm, hard strokes and Blake's fervent kiss that had developed a life of its own, orgasm gripped her and she shuddered in her mates' embrace.

She broke away from Blake's mouth. "Fill me. All of you."

"I think the lady wants us." Blake grinned crookedly. He was the only one with clothes left on, and he stripped them off fast. His cock jutted out from its tangle of blond curls, thick and proud.

Mac crawled onto the bed and tucked a pillow behind his back. He splayed his legs wide and teased his hard on with nimble fingers before crooking them her way.

Sophie didn't wait for a second invitation. She all but dove onto his erection, wriggling to seat him firmly inside her. Mac shut his eyes and made a very satisfied male sound before wrapping his hands around her waist.

Blake knelt behind her. Reaching between her legs, he gathered some of her juices, presumably to lubricate his cock. He strung kisses down her backbone until he reached her ass. Teasing first with his fingers and then with the head of his cock, he moved just past the entrance to her anus. She scootched back to make the angle easier for the cock inside her and the one that wanted in.

"That's my girl." Blake's hot breath scorched her back, and he eased himself farther inside.

Gideon tweaked and teased her breasts and her clit. She reached for his engorged flesh, but changed her mind. "Can you arrange yourself so I can get your penis into my mouth?" Sophie took a deep breath and repeated the words since the first batch came out garbled.

Bending to brush his lips over hers, Gideon murmured, "I'm pretty sure that can be arranged. Let me get some pillows from one of the other beds."

Mac thrust faster, setting a rhythm with his hands on her hips. Blake sank full length into her and wrapped his arms around her, cupping her breasts in both hands. Desire thickened the air as the men's magic rose. The scents of evergreen forests and dry, desert heat filled the room.

Gideon cradled her head in his hands and turned her so his cock butted against her mouth. She gripped his shaft and held tight while she licked and laved the velvety tip of him, loving the salty taste of semen dribbling out.

Her belly tightened with pure, unslaked lust. Blake was thrusting harder, and he moved a hand from her breast to between her legs where he teased her clit, walking her along an edge of pure sensation, without allowing her to tumble over into release.

She grazed Gideon's shaft with her teeth and pumped hard with her hand. He swelled in her mouth, thrilling her beyond measure, and she worked him harder. He tried to pull away, clearly at the edge of climax, but she held tight. She wanted him to come in her mouth. Wanted the others to spill their seed in her body too.

With a sensual groan, the cock in her hand quivered and spurted, sending gouts of salty semen into her waiting mouth. Blake drummed his fingers on either side of her clit and the climax he'd been keeping a hairsbreadth away from her slammed home, flattening her with its intensity. He kept rubbing, and she kept coming.

"Now." Blake cried. "Now!" Deep in her anus, his cock juddered as he released.

"Too much peer pressure." Mac laughed deep and low and she felt him come, drowning her pussy with scorching fluid.

She still had Gideon's cock in a death grip, and he pried her fingers loose. "That was incredible. Thank you. I tried to get away before I came."

"But I wouldn't let you." Sophie was panting hard, and her heart still hammered a rhythm against her ribs. Even though the last string of climaxes almost made her pass out, if Blake kept rubbing her, maybe she could come one more time.

He pulled out of her and Mac lifted her off his cock. Something passed between the men, and she knew they were communicating telepathically. Before she could focus magic to listen in, Blake headed for the bathroom.

"Need to wash off," he called over a shoulder.

"We know you said one round," Mac smiled winningly. "But that was for us. We'll quit right after we clean you up nicely."

"I can follow Blake into the bathroom and get my own washcloth." She squirmed, telling her newly awakened sexuality to settle down.

"It wasn't a cloth we had in mind." Gideon scooped her off Mac's splayed legs and laid her on the bed. Mac moved so he could fondle her breasts and Gideon closed his mouth over her clit. He slid two fingers inside her, tantalizing her while he sucked hard on her swollen, sensitive nub.

The arousal she'd tried to defeat rushed in like gangbusters, and the room exploded in craving for her mates. Mac crushed his mouth over hers and plumbed her mouth with his tongue while moving from one breast to the next. Gideon fucked her with his fingers while sucking on her. She buried her hands in his hair and pressed hard against his questing mouth. Before the world swirled out of control, Blake was there, fondling her breasts and urging Gideon on.

"She's almost there, brother. I feel her heat. Do her harder and she'll come."

Gideon did indeed suck harder, and she melted around his mouth and fingers as climax racked her. The men were amazing, leading her from peak to peak until there was truly nothing left.

Somehow they ended up all laying together, with the men's arms around her and the music of their endearments filling her ears.

"I'm happy," she murmured. "Happier than I ever thought I'd be."

"We'll move heaven and earth to keep you that way," Blake said, sounding fierce.

She drifted for a while, not asleep, but not quite awake, either. Something nagged her, though, dragged her from the pleasant place where her mates cradled her.

Tomorrow.

She had to see if her gift could help her mates and the wolf shifters who'd be with them. Sophie twisted away from the warmth of her mates' bodies. Crawling over a leg here and an arm there, she finally ended up sitting on the edge of the bed.

"What is it?" Gideon asked.

"If you need something," Blake chimed in, "we can get it for you."

Tenderness cracked open and spilled through her. "This is one thing you can't do for me. I'm going to rinse off, and then I'm going to get dressed and go outside."

"That can wait until morning," Gideon said. "You need your rest." Protectiveness underscored his words.

"No," she said. "It can't. The moon will help. So will darkness. My power is strongest then."

"We'll go with you." Blake flowed to his feet, lithe and graceful.

"It's really not necessary—" she began.

"In a pig's eye, it's not," Mac said. He stood too and began hunting through the piles of discarded clothing for his.

Sophie headed for the bathroom where she dragged a warm washcloth over her face and hands and between her legs. She was deliciously sore, but if she didn't sense the urgency of calling a vision, she'd keep right on making love.

"Will you want to use the same spot you used earlier today?" Blake asked.

She nodded. "It's a vortex. I found it shortly after I got here. Or it found me. Maybe it's because of my Indian blood, but I sense places that concentrate and amplify energy."

"I'll go do what I can to prepare it for you." Blake started for the door.

"Hang on." Sophie caught up to him before he got there.

"You can't come with me," he pointed out. "You're still naked."

She rolled her eyes. "Tell me something I don't know. Be careful of the vortex. If you can sense it and not disturb its power with your own, fine. If not, it's best to leave it alone."

"I'll lead with my magic." Blake kissed her forehead and turned to leave.

She watched the door close behind him and then looked for her clothing. The men had laid it out on the rumpled bed. "Aw, thanks." She pulled on her underwear and followed it with her skirt, blouse, and sweater. Lastly, she sat to put on her boots.

"We're going to see if we can help Blake," Gideon said.

"He told us he'd be in the herb garden," Mac added.

"I'll be right behind you," she said, still lacing her boots.

Sophie gazed after her mates and then got to her feet. The room reeked of sex and heat and satisfaction. She inhaled deeply, wanting as much of her mates' essence as she could absorb. The next hour might bring answers she'd rather not have, but she couldn't stick her head in the sand, either.

The goddess had graced her with the gift of foreseeing. It had stood her in good stead with her brother—along with her spells praying for his demise. If it helped the men she loved, the men mated to her through an ancient bond she was only now beginning to sense and appreciate, she had to use it.

No choice. Not really.

Sophie let herself out into the dark, silent corridor. When she opened her magic, she sensed the other two shifter families lost in the magic of loving one another. A soft smile curved her lips as she remembered lying in bed and hearing everyone but her making love. It had been the beginning of her sexual awakening, and it arrived exactly when she needed it most.

Humming softly, she began to gather power around her like a

shining cloak. She took the same route she had earlier. The study's door led to the back of the house and was much closer to the herb garden than going out the front entrance. Sophie felt the men's magic before she saw them. It eddied softly against the blackness of full night. Dawn was hours away yet, and the timing was perfect for calling magic.

When she came through the gateway into the herb garden, three coyotes greeted her, pushing warm, wet snouts into her hand and nuzzling her. Sophie buried her hands in their rough pelts. "I felt you, but I didn't expect…" She let her words trail off.

"Our magic is strongest this way." Blake's deep voice rippled through her mind.

"But is it safe for you?" She answered the same way.

"Safe enough so long as none of us break into howls or yips." Understated humor ran beneath Mac's words.

Sophie bent and kissed the tip of his black nose. The other two crowded close, so she kissed them too before settling on the same flat rock she'd used earlier. Clearly someone besides her had sensed the vortex and positioned the rock so they could take advantage of it to summon their own power.

"Stay out of my mind," she cautioned. *"There's only room for one on these trips."*

Closing her eyes, she hummed and started the staccato finger pattern to bring her trance. After blessing the earth mother, she emptied her mind and opened herself to the future. Specifically the future for the three coyote shifters ranged about her like furred sentinels, staunch against anything that might harm her while she sat helpless in trance.

Familiar gray clouds swirled around her, piquant with the scents of burning herbs. It was why she'd picked the herb garden in the first place, never suspecting the vortex until she called on her power here and found it by accident.

When the clouds cleared, coyotes and wolves romped along a steep mountainside. As with many of her visions, the terrain was nothing like anything on earth. A violet sky stood stark behind jagged peaks crested with pale green snow. The animals were clearly playing with one another, having a carefree frolic, when one of the wolves stopped dead, fell back on his haunches and howled.

A coyote lunged for the wolf and batted a paw across his muzzle. The wolf drew back his upper lip, snarling, but then he lapsed into silence. Shadows crept across the mountainside, blotting out the violet patina from that unnatural sky. The wolves and coyotes formed a rough circle facing outward. Their hackles raised menacingly as they took a stand against foul energy approaching.

With no warning, the earth beneath the animals erupted, sending clods of dirt and rocks many feet into the air. Men raced from subterranean caverns wielding primitive tools. Cudgels and maces flew from their hands, but they had swords and knives as well.

Sophie's heart hammered, but she held onto her vision. If she became upset, it would fritter away like yesterday's moonbeams. Men just kept flowing out of the earth and fell upon the animals. The contest seemed impossible. So many men, and only a few animals. Blood flowed, its coppery scent cloying in her nostrils. She squinted to see through the melee of flying dust, bodies, and blood jetting feet into the air from severed vessels.

As quickly as it had formed, her vision quieted. Sophie bit on her lower lip until the hot taste of blood told her it was enough. She waited, barely breathing. What would be left? Would the goddess gift her with that information too?

Finally, when her stomach was twisted so tight, she was certain she'd vomit, animals formed in front of her eyes. And men's bodies. Lots of them sprawled across dirt and rocks. The mountainside had vanished, replaced by an endless vista of mud-choked dirt.

Please.

Sophie mouthed a silent prayer and peered at the animals walking slowly back and forth. Three coyotes were still on their feet. The intensity of her relief nearly drove her from trance, but she wasn't done. Eight wolves. Where were the eight wolves? No matter how many times she counted, there were only seven.

She scanned the field, hunting for a fallen wolf, hoping he was only injured, not dead, but couldn't find him. When what that meant slammed into her, she clawed her way out of trance. Nothing elegant here. No gradual transitions.

She forced her eyes open. Her mates, still in coyote form, regarded her through worried eyes. *"Shift,"* she urged.

The air in the herb garden flashed so bright with power, she shielded her eyes.

Arms closed around her as her mates embraced her, sensing her desolation.

"Get dressed," she said. "And then we need to go inside where we won't be overheard."

The men scrambled back into their clothes. "Do I need to get Jed?" Blake asked her.

"Good idea. It will save time."

As she made her way back to the study, Sophie picked through what she'd seen. Visions spoke in symbols, which meant they were subject to interpretation, but she was fairly certain of what she'd witnessed. By the time Blake bolted into the study with Jed in tow, she knew exactly what she needed to tell the shifters.

Mac and Gideon were worried about her. She'd felt the weight of their concern walking inside, but hadn't responded to it other than to reassure them she was fine.

Jed belted a dark blue robe more firmly around him. When he faced Sophie, his face was set in grim lines, but his eyes were kind. "Blake says you volunteered to look into the future for us. Thank you. What did you see?"

"Visions aren't like watching a movie—" she began.

"I don't need that part," Jed cut in. "I'm not trying to be rude, but give us the gist of your vision."

She outlined it, followed with, "What I think it means is that the Hunters' headquarters are in the San Gabriels. Otherwise there wouldn't have been so many of them. You need to take more men with you. The other thing is one wolf was missing at the end. Since I didn't find his body, my guess is Hunters took him prisoner."

"What did the wolf look like?" Jed asked tightlipped.

"It's not so much what someone looks like as how they feel in vision states," she replied. "The only wolf energy that was missing at the end was yours."

Jed narrowed his eyes to slits and focused intently on Sophie. "Whatever you do, do not tell Alice that. I won't have her worry the whole time I'm gone."

Sophie inclined her head in respect. "You might end up their prisoner. I'm impressed that your first concern is your mate."

"Damn straight." Jed pounded a fist down on a table, making things rattle. "I'm going to wake the rest of the men, or roust them out of their mated bliss. We need to rethink tomorrow."

"We'll take you back to our room," Blake told Sophie. When she raised a brow, he went on, "No women at our war councils."

Jed paused in the doorway and looked back at her. "Thank you. Thank you very much. You've validated my instincts to spare your life many times over."

"You're welcome."

She turned to her mates once Jed was gone. "I'm almost ashamed how relieved I was once I discovered all three of you made it through tomorrow alive."

"We'll make certain Jed comes through in one piece too," Blake said gruffly. He offered his arm, but she shook her head.

"You have enough to worry about. I can find my own way to my room."

Her mates kissed her, and she made her way out into the darkened hall. At first, she started for her room on the third floor, but then she changed directions. It was unlikely the men would return to their shared bed tonight, but if they did, she wanted to be there. Worry vied with love. Her mates would probably be safe, but she remembered the wild look in Alice's eyes when she'd vowed retribution if anything happened to any of her men.

Sophie inhaled raggedly. Nothing in visions was certain. What she'd seen would've come to pass, but she'd thrown a clod into the churn by telling the men. They'd alter the energy they brought to the battle, so the outcome might well change too.

Though she didn't feel sleepy, she slid out of her clothes and tucked herself into a bed still warm from their earlier lovemaking. With the scents of her mates eddying around her, she fell into an uneasy doze, inviting the dream world to bring her more information.

CHAPTER 14

arly Evening, San Gabriel Mountains

Blake stole from one boulder to another, keeping to shadows as much as he could. He'd muted his energy down to nothing. All of them had. In all, twenty-five shifters comprised today's mission. Three coyotes, three bears, three mountain cats, and sixteen wolves. The eight from Jed's house, plus an additional eight who lived close and that he'd summoned on very short notice. Jed was *de facto* leader. Blake was his second, and Keir third in line.

A short forty-five minute drive brought them to within striking distance of the landmarks from Sophie's vision. The San Gabriels bordered Los Angeles to the north, and if his mate's information was accurate, the Hunters' headquarters was located about five miles up a snaking network of dirt roads.

Hiding the cars had proven impossible, so they'd staggered where they left the five vehicles, rather than parking all of them next to each other, and tucked keys beneath tires. No one knew exactly who'd return, and it made sense to have the vehicles available to everyone. Despite Jed's original plan to leave early in the morning, they'd waited until late afternoon. There were enough of them, they needed darkness to shield their movements.

This had turned into something far beyond the originally conceived reconnaissance mission. Blake assumed the mountains would run red with Hunter blood before the night was out. Grim satisfaction filled him. Retribution was long overdue.

Except there weren't any handy glaciers to conceal the bodies this time.

He eyed the darkening sky and grimaced. No clouds to hide the moon. It wouldn't be up for a few hours, but it was close to full and its light impossible to avoid. Gideon and Mac paced him in front and behind. They were approaching their target from the four directions native to their clans, which meant coyotes were circling to move in from the east. Rather than have all sixteen wolves converge from the west, Jed split them up, assigning four wolves to each clan.

Blake sent a cautious tendril of power outward, seeking the wolves traveling with him. He found Les and Karl easily, but not the others. They were supposed to keep communication to bare bones minimum, so he didn't call them. There'd be time to track the missing wolves later—if he had to. Likely, they were just shielding themselves, much as he was. The more he thought about it, the more probable it seemed. It was easy for him to pick up on Les and Karl's emanations since he knew them.

Jed hadn't said much about the possibility of being kidnapped by Hunters, but then he didn't have to. If they caught him, they'd bind him with iron to mute his power down to nothing and torture him.

Blake curled his hands into tight fists. That would *not* happen. Not now. Not ever. Jed was a talented alpha, the most levelheaded of them, and shifters couldn't afford to lose him.

Gideon sidled next to him. "Only another mile," he whispered next to Blake's ear.

Blake understood his meaning well enough. Time to gather his small troupe and finalize their plans. He let out a low yowl, duplicate to any coyote anywhere. It was the signal for his men to come together. He picked a large boulder and sheltered in its lee, waiting.

Mac, Les, and Karl faded out of the growing darkness. Soon the other two wolf shifters trotted up. "Sorry," one of them mouthed. "We thought we were being followed, so we got off the road."

"Did you actually see anyone?" Blake asked.

Both of the wolf shifters were tall with long, dark hair and dark eyes. The more muscular of the two shook his head. "Unfortunately, no. It was more a feeling we were being watched."

Blake thought about it. "If this really is their headquarters, I'd post sentries. Wouldn't want any surprises."

Les bent closer within the tight circle of men. "Should we track and kill? If we shift, we'll figure it out soon enough."

"It's breaking protocol," Blake said.

"If there is a sentry and he's on his way right now to warn everyone, it's in our best interest to cut him off," Karl argued.

Blake ground his teeth together. The plan had been for all of them to get within a mile of the place, shift, and then attack the compound. They were close enough, they could justify taking down a Hunter.

He met each man's gaze and held it for a moment. "Remember. No blood if you can help it. Kill so you silence them. We don't want any screams, either. If you see Jed, protect him."

"Easier said than done." Les chuckled grimly. "Hard to protect the man when he sees himself as invincible."

Blake began shucking his clothes. The other men did the same. If they somehow came through tonight in one piece, they'd need their clothing. Everyone thought shifters committed murder by the light of the moon, and being naked wasn't wise. He wadded his clothes under a few rocks and hid them as best he could. Shoes too.

Once all of them were naked, he cautioned. "One last thing. Telepathy only if the straights are dire. Coyotes pack up. Wolves pack up. We don't run together in nature, so we won't run together up here, either. If we get goddamned lucky, there won't be some happy "normal" hunters sitting in blinds, hoping for our pelts for a cap."

"What about the sentry we thought we sensed?" One of the wolves asked.

"We'll hunt for him," Karl said. "If we find him and kill him, one of us will howl once."

"Good hunting. Let's do this," Blake commanded. He wanted to get the operation underway. The sooner they got moving, the sooner he, Mac, and Gideon would be back by Sophie's side.

They shifted one by one. The light flashes weren't quite so blinding that way. His senses flooded with enhanced information, and he took to the open countryside at a brisk trot. No more reason to stick to the road. Four feet were much more agile than two, and his night vision as a coyote much sharper. He and his lieutenants hadn't been on the move for more than a few minutes when a lone wolf howl split the air.

Mac shoulder butted him, but held silence. So there had been a sentry. Tracking was trivial in their animal forms, and the poor sod never stood a chance. Approval burned through Blake. One less Hunter meant they were one step closer to freedom for Shifters. Maybe not freedom—not exactly—but at least one less fucker to deal with, who had shifters in his gunsights.

Muted lights flared ahead. A large building sat well back from the road. Blake turned hard right to circle it, get the lay of things. It turned out to be more than one building as he grew closer. More like an enormous gated compound with a large, primary structure made of stone and multiple smaller buildings constructed from lumber. A tall fence surrounded everything, maybe a quarter mile on each side. Metal bars mounted with floodlights were interspersed with wood, and rolling barbed wire graced the top. Blake wondered if the fence carried an electric charge. It could pose a problem if it did.

Mac and Gideon drew next to him, and Blake sensed the other shifters approaching from all sides. The safest path would be vaulting over one of the gates. They wouldn't be electrified. He sent a small jot of power outward to augment his sensitive nose. Because he didn't like the answer, he risked doing it once more. And came up with the same information.

Over a hundred Hunters were inside the compound. Four to one weren't bad odds, but they'd need to attack as a group, not separately, to deal with such a large number. Blake risked a burst of telepathy, aimed at Jed. *"Too many."*

Jed's answer was immediate. *"My take too. Everyone circle to the back gate."*

Blake settled into an easy lope with his lieutenants by his side. Just as they rounded the rear corner of the compound, lights flared, effectively blinding him.

Shit! Hunters must've heard our mind talk.

Marshaling his power, Blake sent it spiraling toward the nearest lamp, shattering it. Around him, other shifters did the same. They'd obviously been discovered, so sheltering their power didn't matter anymore, which meant they could blow the nearest gate by focusing the same power that was obliterating the lights.

He heard the click of metal against metal moments before weapon fire blasted from inside the compound. Many of the bullets plowed into the fence, but some made it through. He dug his claws into soft earth and raced for the gate, intent on annihilating it to give them entrance.

Jed beat him to it. By the time Blake and his lieutenants covered the last quarter mile, the rear gate stood open, and shifters streamed inside.

"Kill fast and clean," Jed's voice sounded.

Bullets flew past Blake. He heard the muted whine of shifters taking hits and leapt on a Hunter with a rifle tucked hard against one shoulder. The man swung his gun to fire, but Blake drove him to the ground and clawed out his eyes. The man screamed once before Blake silenced him by breaking his neck.

No need for stealth. No need for silence, either. Not with all the gunfire and men shrieking their fury as shifters took them out. He picked his next target fast and hit him hard from behind. As soon as the man hit the dirt, Blake closed his jaws over his spinal column, severing it. There'd be blood, but not much. The stench of death grew as men's bladders and bowels released. Battlefields always smelled the same, like victory. Because he couldn't help it, revenge drove a single howl, but just one. Celebration would happen after they won.

Adrenaline hummed hot through his veins as bloodlust took over. He killed two more before something heavy landed atop him, rolling him to the ground. Blake grappled with the Hunter, biting and pawing, but the man held him from behind with his neck in a death grip. Blake understood. When their bullets weren't working, the Hunters were trying to break their necks, just like he'd been doing to them.

No help for it. He needed hands. As he hoped, the blinding flash from him shifting shocked his assailant enough for him to loosen his grip. Blake twisted in his grasp and as soon as he had fingers, he jammed them into the man's eyes. One quick, hard jab before he closed his strong hands around the man's neck and squeezed until he heard vertebrae snap.

Satisfying to kill this way, up close and personal. He scanned the field. Still plenty of Hunters on their feet, but not nearly as many as at the beginning. Morphing back to coyote, he circled behind one man and took him down as a flurry of bullets sprayed from his gun.

Time to see how everyone else was doing. *"Team coyote, report in."*

Mac and Gideon raced to his side, bellies low to the ground as they zigzagged to avoid gunfire. Les, Karl, and the other two wolves slunk from shadows behind him. Blake took stock. One of the wolves was limping.

"How bad?" he demanded.

"Clean shot through my flank," the wolf said. *"Another hour and I'll have it healed."*

"Can you fight?"

"Affirmative."

"Back at it, men. We should have this knocked very soon." Blake picked another Hunter, but a mountain cat leapt on him before Blake got there. The same thing happened with his next target, except a wolf took him out. Since he wasn't needed on the field anymore, he slipped behind one of the smaller buildings where he could shelter and took stock. Had any Hunters slipped out the ruined gate? Or worse, driven out the front? He flipped through his memories. If a car had started up, he might've heard it. Maybe. There'd been so much gunfire at the beginning, he might not have.

Running on instincts, which had rarely failed him, he called for Mac and Gideon.

"Yes, boss?" Gideon glided to his side, a dark shadow against the blackness of the night. Mercifully, clouds had rolled in, obliterating the moon.

"The others have this under control. We're heading back to the road. I want to make certain none of those bastards hightailed it out of here."

"I didn't hear any cars," Mac said.

"You might not have," Gideon countered, mirroring Blake's thoughts from earlier.

"Hang on," Blake said. *"Let me tell Jed what we're about."* He projected his mind voice beyond the space in front of him, calling for Jed.

No answer, so he tried again.

"We don't know where he is," Bron's voice sounded frantic, even through the mind link.

"I'm on it," Blake said. *"Mac, Gid, and I are on our way back to the road."*

"Last Hunter just went down," Terin didn't sound nearly as pleased as he might have. *"Bron and I will search the buildings with the other wolves."*

"Stay in touch," Blake said.

"You too," Bron replied. *"Let us know as soon as you find something."*

Blake took off at a dead run with his lieutenants by his sides. Apparently Sophie's vision was playing itself out since Jed's energy was conspicuously absent. When they came to the main road, he stopped, scenting the air. This was far from the only road crisscrossing these mountains. If they picked wrong, it might mean the difference between Jed living or being subjected to the lethal whims of the madmen, who signed up to be Hunters.

"We should split up," he told the others.

"Agreed," Gideon said. *"We can cover more ground. If one of us scents him, we'll signal."*

"If you find Jed, do not attempt a rescue until all of us are there," Blake cautioned. At nods from his lieutenants, he bolted up the road climbing higher into the mountains. For all he knew, the buildings they'd just left were only part of the Hunters' presence up here. Blake cast his magic in a wide net as he ran, on the lookout for anything, the faintest of clues. He knew Jed's scent and focused intently.

His feet flew over the packed dirt road, covering distance. He was moving so fast, he would've missed a side road entirely if his nose hadn't sounded an alarm. Digging his claws into the dirt, he skidded to a halt, snout raised, snuffling.

Yes!

Jed had come this way, accompanied by at least three Hunters, maybe four. Blake took a hard look at the narrow track leading off the main road. Someone had uprooted sagebrush and dragged it over the entrance. Blake snorted laughter. As if a few bushes could hide something from a shifter, and then he sobered. He'd been so intent on the terrain ahead, he'd nearly missed the piled-up sagebrush. The Hunters were smarter than he gave them credit for. A fact he should keep front and center. Underestimating them wasn't wise.

He raised his muzzle and yipped to signal his lieutenants. What to do about Bron, Terin, and the other wolves? He could reach them, but if he did, he'd surely alert whoever had taken the barely-there road—not more than two divots in the dirt—that led straight uphill.

Mac raced up to him with Gideon not far behind. Both were breathing hard. Blake showed them the way he was certain Jed had gone, and the three coyotes leapt over the sagebrush. Blake slowed on the other side, intent on studying the ground.

"Goddammit! Boots. Not paws. Not bare feet. Boots."

"Jed must be unconscious and they're carrying him," Mac murmured.

"What do you want to do about the other wolves?" Gideon asked.

"Nothing," Blake snapped. *"If we call them, we'll give ourselves away. Shield your presence. Let's get moving."*

They loped uphill for at least a mile before the building Blake figured had to be there came into view. Not fancy like the compound below, this one was small—not more than twenty feet square—and dark, perched on one of the few flat areas to the left of the road. Probably no electricity up here, which was a plus. No lights to deal with. Jed's scent had grown stronger as they climbed, but so had the reek of Hunters.

Blake drew to a halt and inhaled deeply, trying to determine how many Hunters they faced. Was it the handful who'd brought Jed here, or were there others?

Mac and Gideon flanked him. *"Just the four who carried him here,"* Gideon murmured, as if he'd intuited Blake's concern.

"At least this place isn't fenced, but we'll need to be men to break in," Blake shielded his speech and hoped to hell it wouldn't bleed

through. He made his way farther uphill to where two huge boulders would conceal the light that was an inevitable part of their transformation and shifted. Mac and Gideon did the same.

They crept around to the back of the house. Flickering light, probably from kerosene lanterns, shone around the edges of blackout curtains. A shiny padlock latched through a hasp on the door. Obviously the Hunters never used this rear entrance. Blake pulled his men right next to him and spoke low. Another advantage to being human was they could avoid the zing of magic that went along with mind speech.

"I'm going to break the lock with power. Be ready. As soon as it lets go, we swarm inside. Kill immediately. Don't worry about elegant or bloodless. We want those fuckers dead. The first three will be a piece of cake, but the fourth will be out for our blood, and you can bet he's not going to sit around with his thumb up his ass while we kill his buddies."

"You got it," Gideon said.

"We need to hurry." Mac ground his teeth together. "Jed's energy's fading fast."

CHAPTER 15

Blake padded noiselessly toward the rickety steps leading to the cabin's back door. He shielded his energy the best he could until he was within a few feet of his objective. Mac and Gideon stayed back. One shifter might remain undetected. Three was another story. Once Blake was close, he focused a thin beam of power and sent it auguring right at the padlock. The tumblers spun before the hasp gave way.

With Mac and Gideon's energy closing fast behind him, Blake bounded up the steps, yanked the lock and swarmed through the door. Four Hunters sat ranged around a square table in an otherwise bare room. Still in wolf form, Jed lay on the floor, wrapped in thick chains, barely breathing. Shock bloomed on the Hunter's faces, and they scrambled for rifles they'd left leaning against a back wall.

Uttering a guttural growl, Blake took the man nearest him. He didn't waste time choking the bastard, just wrapped his hands around the man's neck and snapped it. Superior shifter strength did the trick. Mac and Gideon killed their targets easily, but none of them were quite quick enough. In the meantime, the fourth Hunter trained a gun on Jed's head.

"I can shoot him quicker than you can kill me," he hissed through clenched teeth.

Blake narrowed his eyes to slits. "True enough. What'd you have in mind?"

The Hunter never removed his gaze from Blake. Short, with thick blond hair, pale blue eyes, and a paunch, he looked to be around fifty. "Not sure. Didn't get that far. Maybe I should just shoot this one anyway." He nudged Jed hard with a booted foot.

"Do that again—" Gideon drew close "—and I'll kill you where you stand. Show some respect."

The Hunter brayed laughter. "You're abominations. All of you. I'd sooner respect the devil."

"Funny, but it's the same way we feel about you," Mac said, his voice deadly quiet.

A loud, snapping sound reverberated through the house. Blake sent power cascading outward, and a satisfied smile spread across his face.

"What was that?" The Hunter looked spooked. Fear rolled off him in noxious smelling waves.

Bron burst through the door at the other side of the building in human form, followed by Terin. Before the Hunter could react, Bron knocked him sideways. Blake dove for the gun, grabbing it about the same time Bron broke the Hunter's neck with a loud crunching sound.

"Aw Jesus." Terin knelt by his alpha. "We've got to get these chains off him." He fingered the padlocks. "I'm afraid if I spring these, the magic will hurt Jed. He's already really weak. Do any of these bastards have keys in their pockets?"

Mac and Gideon scrabbled through the dead men's clothes. "These should do." Mac tossed a large ring sporting several keys Terin's way. It took him several tries, but he finally located the keys that sprang the padlocks.

Bron had positioned himself at Jed's head and was pouring magic into him. Bright white light shimmered, and the air crackled with power. "Get that iron out of here," he ordered. "Outside the cabin. It's interfering with me too."

Terin and Gideon dragged the chains out the open back door. Blake heard them clatter as they slithered to the bottom of the steps. He sat back on his haunches. Jed felt frail to him, too feeble for even the chains to explain things.

"What'd they do to him?" he asked Bron.

"Forced poison down him. Must've injected it since I can't see Jed opening his mouth for them—unless they knocked him unconscious first. Without the chains, he can neutralize it, move beyond it. I hope."

"How'd you find us?" Gideon asked as he and Terin walked back inside.

Terin shot a pointed look his way. "I bet you can always locate your alpha."

"Sorry. Point taken." Gideon rolled his eyes. "Not thinking clearly. Can we help?" He moved closer.

"I sent a man down to bring one of the cars up," Terin said. "Don't think it can make it up this side road, but if we can get Jed down to the junction, we can drive him out of here to where we'll have a better chance of bringing him around. If he can gather enough strength to shift back to human, we'll have it made."

"What about the rest of us?" Blake asked.

"Amazingly, no serious casualties," Terin replied. "They're all on their way out of here. We're the only shifters left on this mountainside."

Blake recognized the importance of getting all of them well clear of the mountains before daybreak. "Do you think any of those slime bags ran the other way? Down the mountain to sound the alarm?"

"We couldn't figure that out," Terin replied. "The whole countryside stank of Hunters and death. Better to ask whoever went for the car. They covered the road below the compound."

Bron pushed to his feet. "Terin. Help me with Jed. Don't jostle him."

"I love him too," the other wolf shifter protested. "You don't need to remind me to be careful."

Blake looked around for something they could use for a litter, but didn't see anything. "Can we help you carry him?"

"No." Bron picked up the front of Jed's body and Terin the back. Together, they moved slowly through the house and out the front door.

"Let's close things up," Blake instructed. "At least that way, doors won't be standing open inviting someone inside to find the dead bodies we're leaving behind."

He and his lieutenants followed the wolf shifters downhill. Blake kept magic deployed on two fronts. He focused on Jed, who at least wasn't getting any weaker, and on whoever might be on the way up the mountain roads with an ugly surprise for them all. They were hideously exposed. The accommodating clouds from earlier had dissipated, leaving them bathed in bring moonlight.

The whine of a car engine struggling with the grade met his ears. "Jesus, but I hope it's one of ours," he muttered.

"It is," Gideon said from a few feet in front. "I wasn't certain, either, until just now. When you get closer, you'll smell wolf."

By the time they got to the road junction, Bron and Terin had already moved Jed into the car's backseat, and it was heading downhill.

"*Sorry.*" Bron's mind voice called back to them. "*Between Jed and me, we took up the whole backseat. No room for three more men.*"

Blake jerked his chin after the car. "Time to be coyotes, men. Run as fast as you can back to our clothes and our cars. We've got to get out of here."

Miles flashed by beneath his paws, and Blake dressed in record time once he shifted. Worry still clotted his veins, thick and viscous, when he slid behind the wheel and ferried the car downhill. He didn't start breathing easier until they passed the turnoff into the San Gabriels.

It was still dark enough, they'd all be back safe at Jed's before dawn. A whole hell of a lot had come down in just a few short hours.

Jed.

He sent up a prayer the wolf clan's alpha would make it. That he'd still been alive after being carried down a mile of rough, rocky ground was promising, but not a guarantee. The first cars he'd seen roared by, missing him by a narrow margin.

"That answers one question," Mac gritted out. "At least one Hunter escaped our net."

Blake turned to gaze after the three cars that had just passed them at breakneck speed. "They were going too fast for you to see or smell anything."

"No one drives that fast at night unless something's gone to hell," Gideon cut in. "I vote with Mac."

"I did see something, though," Mac protested. "Only the lead car had its headlamps on. The others were using its light to travel, which means they were together. And there was only one man in each car, the driver. My guess is they're headed uphill to either clear out incriminating evidence or do something about their dead."

"One problem at a time," Blake said. "Let's get this show home and make sure Jed survives. Then we can tackle the fallout from tonight."

"We did good," Mac said.

"Sure as hell did," Gideon crowed. "God, it felt good to murder those sons of bitches."

It had. Blake's blood still ran hot with the memory of feeling the life drain out of the Hunters he'd personally dispatched. He pushed his elation aside. Survival of his clan came before anything else.

"I'd wipe those smiles off your faces," he cautioned. "Last time, we didn't get caught. We won't be so lucky this time. We left a piss pot of evidence behind for the authorities to cull through. I hope to hell it doesn't lead them right to us."

"How could it?" Gideon demanded.

"Yeah, once we're sure Jed's okay, we'll head right back to Vegas with Sophie," Mac said.

Blake opened his mouth, but snapped it shut. Telling his lieutenants that another location wouldn't shield them from an all-out witch hunt, would come off as patronizing. Let them enjoy tonight's victory for now. The time to pay the piper would come soon enough.

SOPHIE AND MEGAN paced up and down the estate's grounds with Alice, inscribing circles around the house. She'd woken both of them three hours ago, frantic something hideous had happened to Jed. "I feel it," she'd insisted, tapping her breastbone. "The place the mate bond springs from jolted me from a sound sleep. And not in a good way."

At Alice's insistence, the women had gathered in the kitchen. At first they'd sat over a bottle of spirits, but after an hour dripped past with no sign of the men, Alice couldn't sit still any longer.

Sophie wanted to tell her what she'd seen in her vision, but Jed had sworn her to silence. More than anything, she wanted to summon another trance state to see if she could figure out what had actually transpired, except her gift was far more accurate foretelling the future than checking in on the past.

"How do you know it's not Terin or Bron?" Megan asked after being silent for several transits of the large house.

"I can't explain it," Alice replied in a low, tortured voice. "Maybe the closest I can come is this feels just like when Jed was mauled by the mountain cat when he was trying to protect me. I had the same sense of impending doom and helplessness then too."

Sophie wanted to reassure her everything would be all right, but the words stuck in her throat. She didn't want to lie to her friend, and she was far from certain Jed would find his way back to them. Instead, she made low, soothing sounds that she hoped might calm Alice. Saying something like she'd still have two mates wouldn't play well. Sophie wouldn't have liked someone telling her that, if something happened to Blake.

Alice stopped walking and spun Sophie to face her. Her eyes flickered with hope mingled with despair, and they burned like green coals in her pale face. "You know something. I see it in your mind. What?"

Sophie tried to draw away, but Alice held her in place, hands gripping like pincers around her shoulder blades. "I don't know anything. Not really," she stammered to buy herself time to think.

Alice chewed on her lip, but at least she let go of Sophie. "That's it." She snapped her fingers. "Jed told me you can see the future. You saw something."

"Alice!" Megan grabbed her arm. "A car just turned up the driveway."

Alice swallowed hard. The hope flaring in her face was hard to look at before she turned and took off for the front of the house at a full gallop.

"Do you know something?" Megan asked, keeping her voice low.

Sophie leaned close. "Yeah, but I promised Jed I'd hold it secret. Come on." She started for the driveway. "No more waiting. We'll find out what happened."

"Damn! I hope it's not bad news. We're all so newly mated..." Megan's voice trailed off.

Sophie offered a quick hug, and the women started for the front of the house. The car had crested the hill and was just turning its engine off.

Alice shrieked, "Jed! Aw, Jesus, Jed!" just before Bron told her to keep her voice down in such sharp tones it shocked Sophie. Bron was usually sweet and even-tempered, but he'd ordered his mate to shut up. It didn't bode well.

Uttering a quick prayer to the earth mother, she hurried around the corner, ready for anything. Breath whooshed from her. A very shaky, stark naked Jed stood between his lieutenants with Alice clinging to him as if he was her only hedge against being lost forever in the void.

"Let go!" Terin's voice was low, but the words were as pointed as Bron's had been. "We need to get him inside."

"Of course." Alice stepped away and hurried up the steps to pull the front door open.

Bron and Terin essentially lifted Jed up the stairs. He was pasty white. Near the top of the steps, he bent over, racked with dry heaves. Foul-smelling red bile spewed from his mouth.

Sophie knew that smell—sacred thorn apple—and raced up the steps with Megan behind her. "That's poison," she said.

"You be quiet too," Bron snapped. "Get inside. We can shield things from in there."

A fourth wolf shifter Sophie recognized as one of her potential suitors from before she met Blake, slid from behind the wheel. He looked trashed, with deep lines radiating out from his eyes and making divots in his forehead. He hurried up the stairs and helped Bron and Terin move Jed the rest of the way inside.

"Alpha. What do you want me and the other wolves to do today?" he asked Jed. "We can try for cleanup if you need us to."

"Do not return to the San Gabriels under any circumstances," Jed snapped sounding a little more like himself. "Tell everyone to take a vacation. Get out of town for a few days. If you're out of telepathy range, use the phone and call me day after tomorrow."

"You got it, boss."

"Grateful for all your help, bro." Terin dropped a hand on the other wolf shifter's shoulder.

"Just be sure our alpha pulls through," he replied gruffly. "I don't know that I've ever heard anything quite so welcome as his voice from the backseat after you finessed his transformation back to human."

"Jed will be fine," Bron said. "We're past the crisis, and he'll heal quickly now. Question is whether we stay here. We may be right behind you heading out of town, once our car comes back."

As if on cue, headlights lit the broad drive and two more cars pulled up. Sophie dove back through the front door, frantic for her own mates. Megan joined her on the porch. The other woman gripped her arm. "Les and Karl are all right, aren't they? They have to be." Her voice was low, urgent. "I didn't feel anything like Alice did."

Sophie was strung so tight, she couldn't find words to answer, so she sent her magic zinging through the night, grateful beyond words when her mates' energy pulsed from the car just shutting off its lights. Les and Karl were with them. The bear and mountain cat alphas and their lieutenants were in the other car.

She swallowed around a dust-dry throat. "Our mates came through unscathed," she croaked out.

"Thank God." Megan broke into a broad smile, but tears formed in the corners of her eyes revealing the depth of her relief. "Come on." She tugged on Sophie's arm. "Let's go down and greet them."

Sophie stumbled into her mates' arms. Blake, Mac, and Gideon stank of blood and death. "Did it happen like I saw it?" Her voice was muffled against Blake's chest.

"Yes and no." Blake's deep voice rumbled against her hair. "Come inside, sweetheart."

Sophie looked up to see Megan trooping up the stairs between her mates, with the bears and mountain cats right behind them. She nodded her understanding and moved inside with her mates surrounding her.

By the time they got to the great room, liquor and food were flowing freely. Alice had glued herself to Jed's side. He sat on one of the overstuffed sofas lining the room, wrapped in a robe someone had gotten for him.

Sophie had no idea if she was breaking some sort of protocol, but she walked up to Jed and knelt so she could look at him. "What happened? Did my vision come to pass?"

Jed blew out a harsh breath and tipped a whiskey bottle to his lips. "Someone shield this room," he said. "My magic's not recovered enough yet."

"Christ, you're lucky you're still alive," Bron muttered.

"I'll take care of the room," Keir said and power shimmered outward from him in iridescent waves. "I want to hear what happened too."

"Not lucky." Jed sent a meaningful look across the room at his lieutenant. "You're the best healer we have."

"Yeah, but I never want to have to drag you back from death's door again." Bron stalked to his alpha, pried the whiskey from him, and drank deep.

"I'll do my best to oblige." Jed extended his hand for the bottle.

"So you did know about this?" Alice addressed Sophie.

She nodded slowly. "I had a vision, but they don't always come true."

"I asked you point blank—" Alice began.

"And I extracted a promise from her not to tell you," Jed interrupted. "I love you, Alice. Don't be angry at Sophie. I'm sure she felt torn."

"It doesn't matter what I felt or didn't feel." Sophie rocked back on her heels. "What happened?"

Jed drew his brows together. "I'm not sure I'll be able to shed all that much light on it. One minute I was fighting and killing— and having a hell of a raucous time—and the next something heavy hit the back of my head, and I passed out cold. When I came to, I was wrapped in iron chains to mute my power and keep me in my wolf form. I guess I must've growled or something, because the Hunters—four of them, but the ones who rescued me know that—started talking about instituting plan B.

"Next thing I knew, they put me down and stuck a needle into the fleshy part of my upper back leg. I sensed poison, tried to fight against it, but between the iron and the thorn apple, I passed out again."

Blake stepped next to where Sophie hunkered in front of Jed. "Did you overhear anything, anything at all, that might indicate why they picked you?"

"No. I wondered the same thing. Best I could come up with is they figured out I'm one of the alphas."

"Do you think they know who you are as a human?" Blake persisted.

"Sorry." Jed shook his head. "I have no idea."

"They must know something." Sophie spoke slowly. "Or I wouldn't have seen them make off with you in my vision. It was specifically you missing, not simply wolf energy."

"I still think you could've told me," Alice muttered. "We're friends."

"Aw, honey." Sophie's heart broke for the other woman. "I'm sorry."

"I know you are. I understand about keeping your word. I'm just sorry my mate placed you in such a tough position. Choosing between your honor and my pain must've torn you up." Alice sent a pointed look at her mate, but Jed just shrugged.

"Sorry, love. I didn't want you to spend the whole time I was gone worrying yourself sick over me." He took another slug of liquor and followed it with some crackers and cheese someone had piled near him on a plate.

"Still friends?" Sophie asked Alice.

"The best." The other woman smiled at her.

Keir and Jon walked to where Blake stood. "We all need rest," Keir said. "I'm hoping the law won't roust us out between now and noon tomorrow."

"No kidding," Jed muttered. "Paramount should vouch for me, but I won't underestimate the power of a hanging mob out for blood."

Blake considered his next words carefully. "Remember, no one knows about Hunters outside their ranks. The general populace wouldn't agree with chasing anyone down and killing them outright. They're good with dumping us in prison, but that's because it's a theoretically humanitarian solution to something they see as a problem."

"Why not blow the whistle on what the Hunters are doing?" Alice asked.

"We're shifters. Persona non grata. No one would believe us," Jed replied, sounding tired.

"I'm not a shifter," Alice countered.

"Yeah, but you're shacking up with one, which is almost worse," Keir said.

"No," Alice countered. "I'm married to him."

"Don't get your feathers ruffled," Keir muttered. "No disrespect meant."

"We're not going to solve this tonight." Jon, who'd been quiet until now, spoke firmly. "We can't control any of the variables. No one knows what the Hunters will do about tonight. They'd have to reveal the location of their hidden compound, which would leave them open to bunches of questions they'd probably rather not answer."

"Most of their records are still up there," Keir said. "It's what we were after when tonight's operation was just a reconnaissance. Unfortunately, we ended up at cross purposes once Jed was kidnapped, so we only took a handful of files with us when we hightailed it out of there. The rest were in padlocked safes we didn't take the time to spring. As it was, we needed our human forms to carry what we did steal."

"Bet they burn the rest of them," Jon growled. "Yellow-bellied assholes."

"Wonder what percentage we wiped out between the Palisades and tonight," Blake mused.

"Likely we won't find that out anytime soon," Jed said. "Let's all turn in. We can plan better once we're rested."

"By then we'll know if the Hunters have identified us," Jon said. "And we can figure out what to do next."

"Wouldn't we be safer leaving tonight?" Alice asked.

Jed turned to his mate, his eyes on fire with something savage. "I'm not running unless there's no choice. If we do, we'll have carved out a path for the rest of our lives." He glanced at the other three alphas, letting his gaze settle on each man. "I can't force you to live by my decisions. If you disagree, you're free to leave and govern your clans as you see fit."

"I've spent the last hundred plus years on the run," Keir growled. "I'm sick of feeling like a fugitive."

"All I want is peace." Blake drew Sophie to her feet. "Come on, sweetheart. I want to clean up before I join you in bed."

Mac and Gideon fell in on either side of them. "We need to bathe too," Mac said. "Every time I inhale, all I smell is death."

The rise and fall of voices followed them as they left the room and mounted the stairs. "Do you really think the authorities might show up here?" Sophie asked.

"Jesus, God, but I hope not," Blake said.

"I'm with Keir," Gideon cut in. "I'm sick of hiding."

Sophie walked to their room, surrounded by her mates. She wanted to offer up another vision, but it was late and everyone was tired, besides it seemed as if she wouldn't be able to pry anyone out of Jed's house, no matter what popped up from the spirit world. She didn't blame the men. Being labeled a second class citizen—or no citizen at all—rankled. She hadn't liked it as an Indian stuffed onto a reservation, and shifters were ancient, proud. They wouldn't go down without a fight, and she loved them all the more for backing their convictions with action.

Hot water pummeled Blake's body, but it couldn't wipe out the carnage from a few hours before. He'd buried the savagery that was part and parcel of his shifter blood, smothered it for so long, it almost made him uncomfortable. He'd been born in a much bloodier, earlier time. An era when brutality was commonplace. During the intervening centuries, a veneer of civility had replaced cruelty and violence—or at least forced them underground.

He was vaguely aware of first Mac, then Gideon, leaving the bathroom. It gave him more space in the large, walk-in, tiled shower stall, and he threw his shoulders back and turned slowly, letting water run down his body until he couldn't smell blood any longer.

Sophie pulled the glass door open and joined him, tilting her head back until her black and silver tresses streamed with water. He opened his arms, but instead of walking into his embrace, she grasped his forearms and gazed into his eyes.

"What's wrong?" she asked.

Blake met her direct stare. She hadn't asked if anything were amiss. With the instincts of her race, coupled with her magic, she understood he wasn't standing under the shower to get clean.

"Maybe a better question would be, what's right?" He tried for a smile, but it felt forced, so he gave it up for wasted effort. Besides, she'd see through him.

"We're right. You and me and Mac and Gideon."

Guilt shot a spear straight into his heart. "Of course we are, darling. I'm just being selfish, wishing I could spirit you back to our home and forget the rest of the world."

"Maybe we could do that," she retorted. "And even get away with it for a little while, but it's like with my people."

Blake shut off the water and reached for towels he'd hung over the top of the shower enclosure. "Say more about that." He handed her a towel, wrapping it around her body.

She took the other towel and started drying him, blotting water from his chest and back. "When we lost the last of the Indian wars, and white men tried to make us believe they were giving us land out of the kindness of their hearts, some of us—oh hell, probably all of us—knew it was a sham. White men gave us shit land, jammed us into places where they could keep a close eye on our whereabouts. In case anybody got any more ideas about fighting back."

Blake opened the glass door and gestured her through. He grabbed a fresh towel and soaked water from her long hair. "So you think that even if we get some concessions from politicians, it won't be worth much."

"Not exactly." Sophie narrowed her eyes. "My people were split into many tribes. Most of those tribes hated each other. Since we failed to stand together, it was easy for the white man to divide and conquer us." She stopped to take a breath. "Our tribes fought one another long before white men pushed west with their wagons. One of the reasons they saw Indians as a threat was because violence was part of our daily life. It was easy to transfer that violence from the neighboring tribe to a wagon train passing through."

She shook her head. "I'm not making a whole lot of sense. There are lots of reasons we lost status in white men's eyes. Once they saw us as unworthy of respect, we got what they felt we deserved."

"But you weren't undeserving of decent treatment," Blake protested.

"Agreed." She drew herself tall. "There's a lesson in what happened to us, though."

"I hear it, loud and clear. Shifters have to present a united front and not back down." He paused, gathering his thoughts. "But we can't keep doing what we did in the Palisades and tonight in the San Gabriels. Killing may feel satisfying and vindicate us, but it isn't the answer. There are too many of them. Besides violence only leads to more violence."

"How many tonight?"

"I don't know. Lots. When you jump into these things, you can't leave any witnesses, yet some Hunters escaped our net."

"Why do you think that?"

"When we were on our way home—past the turnoff into the mountains, but still where there was no other traffic—cars passed us going really fast. Three of them with one man apiece."

"You believe they were some kind of cleanup crew."

Blake nodded. "I'm sure of it. We haven't seen the last of tonight."

He held out his arms again. This time she walked into them, and when he held her tight against him, she was trembling. Blake stroked her hair. "Don't be afraid, sweetheart. Between the three of us, we'll keep you safe."

"It's not that." Her voice was muffled against his neck.

"What is it, then?"

"I'm angry." She reared back, her midnight eyes burning hot. "What happened to my people was horrible, and so is what's happened to shifters. Indians gave up. Stopped fighting back. Maybe we would've lost, but at least we would've gone down with our pride intact. Instead, we stuck ourselves with white men's ways—and their stupid rules about how to live."

"Better dead than subjugated and turned into pawns?" He drew her head into the hollow of his shoulder again and felt her nod mutely against him.

Mac and Gideon shouldered into the bathroom. "We wondered what happened to you," Mac said.

"We were just talking." Blake glanced at his lieutenants and understood how much they meant to him. How much the shifter way of forming family groups was ingrained in his blood. He didn't want to give it up in favor of assimilating into the dominant culture that Sophie would call white men's rules.

"We've been keeping the bed warm for you." Gideon smiled suggestively.

"Getting lonely out there," Mac added.

Sophie pulled away from Blake and opened her arms. The men surrounded her until everyone was touching. "This is one of the things Blake and I were discussing," she said. "How shifters have created a way of life that works for them. And how it would be anathema to white men. Do you believe for a minute they'll condone something they view as sick and perverted?"

"She's right," Mac muttered.

"Keep talking," Blake urged his lieutenant, sensing there was more to Mac's words.

"Why do you think the Church came up with the idea of training Hunters in the first place?" Mac countered. "To have an instrument to destroy something they saw as an affront to the god they worship."

"Never looked at in in quite that way," Blake said. "Smart of them, though. They develop a secret society, bound by chastity and obedience just like their priests, and send them out to do their dirty work. If any of them were caught or questioned, their vows would force them to hold silence."

"Exactly." Gideon sounded disgusted. "It's how and why Hunters have survived."

"So maybe we're not so far off," Blake said. "Hunters do need to die, but we also need to become visible again. If we don't, we'll be stuck with the status quo we've carved out for ourselves."

"Enough philosophy for one night?" Gideon drew back and quirked a brow.

"Indeed," Mac said. "There's little enough of the night left as it is to enjoy our mate."

The pheromones of their arousal lifted Blake from the dark pit his thoughts had become, but he was still protective of their mate. Tilting her chin with a finger, he gazed into her eyes. "What about it, darling? I know how worried you must've been. Tell us what you need. If it's just for all of us to hold you and soothe you with our magic, we can do that."

"Sorry." Gideon met her gaze too. "I wasn't thinking. What do you need? We'll take care of you."

"Now and always," Mac said.

"I want all of you—now and always." She borrowed Mac's words. "If it's one thing that sank in while I was pacing the gardens with Alice and Megan earlier, it's that we should take advantage of our love and joy at every opportunity."

She grabbed Blake's hand and motioned to Mac and Gideon. "Hurry. I can't wait to feel all of you around me again."

Blake followed Sophie to the large bed butted into a corner of the lavish room. An elaborately carved oak headboard reached for the ceiling, and the matching footboard rose almost as high. Rather than lying down, she moved a padded straight back chair away from a small desk and turned it to face the bed.

"You have something in mind." Blake grinned and wiped his worries about Hunters from their front and center spot in his thoughts.

She grinned back and patted the chair. "Sit."

He did, his cock rising in front of him as he anticipated what might come next. Mac and Gideon swarmed around them.

"Where do you want us?" Gideon demanded.

"Sit on the bed facing Blake."

Sophie knelt on the thick carpet and took Blake's cock into her mouth, licking slowly up his shaft. Heat shot along his nerves and he buried his hands in her thick, wet hair. She licked and sucked and teased, but then she spun on her haunches and took Mac's penis into her mouth, while she closed a hand around Gideon's.

Color rose beneath her coppery skin, turning it a lovely rose tone, as she moved from Mac's cock to Gideon's and back. Grunts and moans of pleasure filled the air, and Blake settled a hand around his cock, stimulating himself as he watched their mate pleasure his pack brothers.

Blake scooted closer and left his chair to hunker on the floor behind Sophie. He reached around her and filled his hands with her breasts, rubbing the erect nipples into even stiffer peaks.

"Whatever you're doing," Gideon gasped, "do more."

"Yeah, the hotter she gets, the harder she works us," Mac managed between panting breaths.

Sophie let go of Mac and Gideon and rocked back against Blake. "Back in the chair," she said, her voice thick with wanting release. "But get it right up next to the bed."

He let go of her and perched on the chair again, positioning it where she'd said. Facing away from him, she sank onto his achingly hard erection, bent her head forward, and continued sucking Mac's and Gideon's cocks. Blake drove into her from behind and wrapped his arms around her, placing one hand on a nipple and sliding the other between her legs.

Caught up in the sexual heat spilling around them, he rubbed her hot, slick nub, feeling it quiver against his hand. Her vault tightened rhythmically around his shaft and he knew she was coming. He didn't hold back. Her pleasure intensified his own and he erupted inside her, riding the crest of his orgasm until it was spent.

Sophie tried to move from Mac back to Gideon, but he gripped her head. "I'm there, darling," he gasped. "Don't leave me now."

Blake felt the heat as Mac came, flooding their mate's mouth with his semen. Gideon's nipples were hard, dark buds, and sexual tension boiled around him as he managed his arousal. Blake knew what he was holding out for.

So did Sophie.

She let go of Mac's cock and let Blake pull out of her body. Free of them, she moved onto the bed and pushed Gideon back so she could straddle him. He made a deep, intensely male sound as she lowered her body atop his. Gripping her hips, he drove hard into her, lost in the scorching heat surrounding his cock.

Blake felt his arousal through their bond, and his cock stiffened again.

Mac moved over. "Go for it," he said through shuddery breaths, still lost in spent passion.

Kneeling behind Sophie, Blake teased the tight bud of her anus with his fingers before setting his cock in place. She moved toward him, welcoming him, so he slid in, keeping the pace slow. It wasn't easy with Sophie's and Gideon's arousal tinging the air with urgency.

Hunger, craving for the woman between them ran like molten silver through his veins. He impaled himself on her upstroke, Gideon on her down stroke. None of them would last long at this rate. Sophie came first, screaming her joy as her body convulsed around the two penises inside her. Gideon released next. Blake felt him spasm through the thin strip of tissue separating their organs.

Blake thought he could ride it through, hold out for another round, but an orgasm boiled up from his balls, catching him by surprise as it took him, spun him around, and wrung him dry.

They ended up in a heap on the bed. Mac crawled beside them and wrapped his arms around everyone as their passion subsided to a warm glow.

"This is so good. All of you are amazing," Sophie said. "How we live is worth fighting for. Don't let anyone take it away from us."

"We love you too, darling," Blake said. Fierce protectiveness roiled through him. He'd pull out every single trick in his book to ensure no one stripped shifters of their lifestyle. No one.

"Maybe we should leave while we can," Gideon muttered.

"It's almost daylight," Mac said. "We'd have to hurry, but we could be out of here before things heated up. If they get ugly, that is."

"We're not deserting Jed and the other alphas," Blake countered. "We stand together."

"Of course, you're right," Gideon agreed. "Sorry. I got caught up in wanting to protect our mate."

"Appreciated," Sophie said. "But I can take care of myself. I've been doing it for a long time now."

"My bristly, little kitten." Blake stroked hair away from her still-flushed face. "We threw down a gauntlet last night. We're going to stand and face whatever happens."

"Just like we always have," Mac said. "Maybe we could get a few minutes' shuteye before the shit hits the fan?"

Sleep didn't seem likely to Blake, but he said, "Good idea. I'll take first watch."

"If there was more of the night left, I'd insist on taking a turn too," Sophie said.

Love for the woman in his arms rose like a tide, and he tightened his hold on her. "Of course, darling. You're part of our pack now."

"Not just humoring me?"

"Never." He kissed her forehead and let his thoughts run free. He wanted to analyze every part of the previous night. Maybe they'd missed something critical.

"Stay with Mac and Gideon," he murmured as he extricated himself from the tangle of bodies splayed across the bed.

"Where are you going?" she asked, sounding much more awake.

"To look at the records we stole from the Hunter compound. It's not wise to leave them in whichever car they ended up in, and I want to see if we got anything that might help us."

"I'll keep watch," Gideon said. "Let us know if you need us."

Deploying his coyote night vision, Blake tossed clothes on and padded from the room, not bothering with shoes.

CHAPTER 17

*J*ed's strength was almost fully returned. Loving Alice, and sharing the energy while his lieutenants made love with her, had switched his focus away from the hell he'd lived through. He was furious he'd allowed himself to be trapped, but every time he replayed what happened, he didn't see how he could've done anything differently. There'd been no warning, none at all. The Hunters who'd sacrificed their lives to hold his attention made certain he wasn't mindful of the ones creeping up from behind. Plus his assailants had shielded themselves so completely, he'd only been aware of them a split second before they clubbed him behind the head, knocking him out.

Early morning light, pearlescent with the promise of the new day, streamed through the windows in their shared bedroom. Everyone had fallen asleep after sex—except him. As he watched the light dance and play with dust motes drifting in the air, an idea surfaced. Careful not to wake anyone, he slipped out of the tangle of arms and legs and made his way quietly across the room and out the door, snagging a robe on his way.

Jed trotted downstairs, glancing at the grandfather clock on the landing as he passed it. Seven straight up. He had time for a quick dip in the pool, and then he'd put his plan into action. He might not need it, but better safe than sorry.

Raising his mind voice, he called the other alphas and asked them to join him in the swimming pool. He was on his third lap when Blake jumped into the water and stroked toward him. Keir and Jon dove in right behind.

"This better be good," Keir sputtered, blowing water as he surfaced.

"I was thinking the same thing." Blake mock-punched Jed's arm. "Back to a hundred percent I see."

"More or less." Jed laughed and slugged Blake back.

"Hey!" the coyote alpha protested. "You dragged me out of my bed—and away from Sophie."

"That may have been true an hour ago, but your energy closed from outside." Jed narrowed his eyes. "What were you doing?"

"Culling through the records in the backseat of Keir's car."

"Shit!" Keir batted a hand on the water's surface, making it splash. "Not that I forgot about them, but good you moved them out of my car. You did move them, right?"

Blake nodded. "Yeah, they're tucked in a back corner of one of the gardens under some stones. Looks like we got at least one, fairly long list of names. Just over five hundred. Not sure how comprehensive it is, or what parts of the country it encompasses. It was coded, but easy enough to break."

"Strong work." Jed nodded approvingly. "Might come in handy."

"Thanks. Back to my original question," Blake said. "What's up?"

"I wanted to run something by all of you before I did it," Jed replied. "I'm going to give Lon Chaney a call in just a minute. I might wake him, but then and again, I might not. He's famous for staying up all night drinking. I'm going to ask if he'll come over here for breakfast and stay through the day."

Blake whistled long and low. "Sweet. He's our alibi."

"The one who can vouch we were here all night," Keir cut in.

Jon grinned from ear to ear. "I like it, except doesn't that mean you'll have to bring him in on what happened? And tell him about us?"

Jed hoisted himself up onto the pool's edge and shook water from his hair. "He already knows what we are, and he's held that information in confidence for the better part of fifteen years. I'm not thinking he'll rat us out now. Beyond that, I wasn't planning to divulge any details about last night. Safer if he doesn't know."

Jed looked at the other three alphas, and they all gave him a thumbs up signal. "I was fairly certain you'd agree," he said, "but I wanted to make sure." He eyed Blake. "You can run on back to your new mate now."

"I'm pretty sure she's in the kitchen scaring up breakfast. Thanks for the thought, though. Once we have a direction and know which way the wind is blowing, Mac, Gideon, and I will head back to Nevada with Sophie. I'm anxious to get her settled in her new home."

"Good idea," Keir said.

"Yup. The more normal we look, the closer we stick to our usual routines, the better," Jon said and then added, "I was planning to drive back to North Dakota with my guys."

"Waldo, Brune, and I were talking last night about how much we missed our mate," Keir said. "We're anxious to get home too."

"At least you all have mates," Jon sounded bitter. "My lieutenants and I are still waiting for the magic to find us."

Compassion for his fellow alpha filled Jed. "I remember Corinne."

"Thank you for that." Jon raised sad, dark eyes. "She's been gone for a long time, but we still miss her."

"When did you lose her?" Keir asked, suddenly somber.

"1720. The last year plague swept through Marseille." Jon's voice cracked with emotion. "We tried to save her, and for a while it looked like she might make it, but we couldn't keep enough blood in her to balance what she was losing." He raked a hand through his red-streaked dark hair. "It doesn't matter, but I never thought hundreds of years would go by without even a hint of a new mate bond."

"Your family group will find a new mate." Jed infused reassurance into his voice. "I'd given up too. So had Bron and Terin, but then Alice came along and voilà! Keep the faith. Miracles do happen. I'm off to call Chaney. Meet you in the kitchen."

Jed toweled off quickly and wrapped the robe back around himself before making his way one floor up to the study. He settled into his desk chair behind an enormous mahogany desk, picked up the black telephone receiver, and dialed a number he knew by heart.

Lon Chaney Jr. answered on the second ring, his voice gravelly from cigarettes and booze. "This fucking better be good, the sun's barely up."

Jed chuckled. "Funny, but you're the second one who's said that to me this morning."

"Jed, you old son of a gun." Lon Chaney paused, clearly thinking. "Did something happen?"

Jed silently blessed him for watching his words. No one ever knew for sure if their phone was being bugged by the FBI. J. Edgar Hoover was notorious for his questionable surveillance tactics.

"Mighty quiet," Chaney observed. "You still there?"

"Yeah. How about breakfast over here?"

"On my way. Wouldn't miss it for the world. Say, my pal, Mr. Z, is with me. Mind if I bring him along?"

Jed knew who Chaney meant. There was only one Mr. Z. Adolph Zukor was the outgoing head of Paramount Studios, where Jed worked as a production manager. "Is he your new drinking buddy?" Jed asked to buy a moment's thinking time.

"Not usually, but he had a blowup with his wife. You know how it is."

"I'm not sure—" Jed began. It might be hard to say anything with Zukor around, but the man was extremely liberal. As a Jew run out of Hungary by anti-Semitic propaganda, he had to be.

"He knows," Chaney said without preamble. "And before you blow a gasket, he figured it out on his own. Insofar as I know, I'm the only one he's discussed it with."

"Goddammit, Lon. You shouldn't have—"

"Starnes!" Chaney broke in, cutting off the rest of Jed's words. "Think about it. Adolph's been persecuted nine ways from Sunday. He's not one to run his mouth to anyone—about anything. Besides, if this is what I think it might be, two of us are better than one."

"Fine," Jed growled. "See you soon."

The connection clicked off, and he stared at the receiver. If Zukor knew and Chaney knew. How many others were aware he was a shifter? He ground his teeth in frustration, but it wasn't a question he was likely to come up with an answer for anytime soon, so he headed upstairs to roust Bron and Terin.

Dressed and ready for the day, Alice was headed out their door as he pulled it open. She wrapped her arms around him. "Aw gee, if I'd known you were coming back to bed, I wouldn't have been in such a hurry to get up."

"She says that to all the guys," Bron called from deeper inside the room.

"Yeah, she got us up a quarter of an hour ago," Terin chimed in. "In truth, we were too keyed up to sleep any longer—or do much of anything else."

Jed herded Alice into the room and shut the door. Next he draped magic around them to shield his words. "Chaney's on his way over. If the authorities show up, he can say he's been here since early afternoon yesterday." Jed inhaled raggedly. "Zukor's with him."

"What the hell?" Terin asked. "Chaney knows about us, but how will this go down with Zukor here?"

"That's just it," Jed said. "Zukor knows too." He held up a hand before the others could pepper him with questions. "According to Lon, Adolph figured things out on his own. He knows how close Chaney and I are, so he asked him about his suspicions."

"Not sounding good," Bron muttered.

"I was shocked too," Jed countered. "And we won't know more until they show up. I'm actually just guessing about the last part. I have no idea why Zukor hit Chaney up for information about us."

"If both of them know, how many others?" Alice asked. She chewed her lower lip, something she did when she was nervous.

"Good point," Bron said.

"Yeah, and not a question we can answer," Terin muttered.

"We're not going to tell them anything about either the Palisades or last night," Jed cautioned. "Only thing they need to know is they arrived around noon yesterday, and we've had a nonstop poker game ever since."

"Got it," Bron said. "Need to get tables set up and scatter some chips around."

"I'll help." Terin nodded. "Come on, Alice. Let's get some coffee before everyone gets here."

"I'm staying with Jed until he's dressed," she replied. "Pour me a cup, though. I'll be there soon."

Jed watched his lieutenants open the door, walk through, and shut it behind them. He wound his arms around Alice. "Try not to worry, love. If the law shows up here, Chaney and Mr. Z are as solid an alibi as we're likely to get. No one will bother us after those two vouch they've been here the last twenty-four hours."

Alice kissed him lightly and stepped away so he could get into something other than the robe he'd worn since he got out of bed. He slid into a pair of dark slacks, a white button down shirt, and a pale green cashmere sweater. Alice fixed a set of gold cufflinks at his wrists and handed him a hairbrush.

"Good call." He looked askance at her as he brushed his hair away from his face and secured it with a tie at the base of his neck. "Will I do?" He held out his arms to his sides.

"You're perfect. Amazing. Yesterday when I was certain you were dead, I—"

"Hush." He placed two fingers over her mouth. "Bad luck to even think such things. Come on, sweetheart. Let's see what we can gin up for our guests for breakfast."

~

"You need not have concerns about me." Adolph Zukor's deeply accented voice rang with truth, and Blake relaxed, but only a little. In his experience, the only way anyone could keep a secret was if they were dead.

"Yes, but how did you figure things out?" Keir persisted.

The slightly built Hungarian set his fork down and winked. "Before I forget entirely, this was a most excellent breakfast." His dark eyes twinkled as he looked from Megan to Sophie to Alice.

"Don't give me a shred of credit," Alice said. "All I did was make the second pot of coffee."

"I still want to know the answer to my question," Keir persisted.

"Easy enough." Adolph met Keir's direct gaze. "Where I come from, I am used to lurking behind the scenes, listening in where I should not. I learn much that way." He took a sip of coffee. "Even though Jed and Lon were circumspect, it was not hard to read between the lines of some of their conversational material."

"Why didn't you ask me?" Jed skewered Adolph with both the full force of his gaze and a smattering of magic meant to tease out truth. Blake saw the spell shimmer in the air.

"You were my employee. I did not wish to make you uncomfortable." Adolph shrugged. "Even though this information is new to you, I have known about…things for many years. And have kept the information strictly confidential beyond a few words shared with Lon." He leaned forward. "Now that you know that I know, I would love to discuss some of the details, though—"

"A car just pulled up at the end of the driveway," Jon said.

Blake straightened in his chair. The others did too.

"You all look like marionettes." Lon Chaney kept his voice low. "Go back to the way you were a minute ago. Smile, chat, appear *normal*, for chrissakes."

The front doorbell rang with all the subtlety of a shotgun blast tearing through the room.

Lon surged to his feet with a bright smile. "I'll answer the door. After all, I'm the bona fide actor here."

Blake leaned toward Sophie, chatting of inconsequentials, but most of his mind was focused on the conversation unfolding in the front hall. His coyote senses amplified a conversation that would've eluded human hearing.

"Why, officers," Chaney boomed. "Whatever can I do for you?"

"Lon Chaney!" The officer sounded nonplussed. "Didn't expect to find you here."

"We sure didn't," a second male voice chimed in.

"Is this a social call?" Chaney persisted. "There's still breakfast left, boys. Come on in and have some coffee and sweet rolls. Omelet's still left too, and bacon and ham."

"Is, um, Mr. Starnes at home?" the first officer asked.

"Indeed. He's in the dining room," Chaney answered. "Come on in, boys." He lowered his voice conspiratorially. "I'll never tell if you take a breather from protecting the good citizens of Los Angeles to break bread with us."

Jed must've decided it was a good time to make an appearance because he trotted out the dining room door. "Morning, fellows!" Jed's distinctive voice rang out. "You're just in time for breakfast."

"Where were you last night?" the second officer blurted.

"Why we were all right here." Chaney did a stellar job of infusing puzzlement into his words. "Zukor's here too. We've had a marathon poker tournament cooking since early afternoon yesterday. Why? Is anything wrong?"

"Nah. We just got bad info," the first officer said. "Sure, we'd be glad to take a load off for a few. Lead out."

"Yeah, we sure did get bad info," the second officer muttered. "Someone fed us a mountain of bullshit."

"Don't bitch," the first one told his associate. "Not often we get a free breakfast out of the deal."

"Hell," Chaney cut in. "If you can stay for a hand of poker, you'd be welcome for that too. You men work your asses off."

The voices drew closer as the group walked toward the dining room.

"Let me walk through introductions." Jed materialized in the doorway, with Chaney and two uniformed policemen right next to him. "This is my wife, Alice." He beckoned her to his side and introduced the rest of them, using first names.

Sophie got to her feet and dished up plates for the men, setting them in front of empty spots at the huge table that could have sat twenty. "Coffee, fellows?" she inquired with an engaging smile.

Blake sat back while Adolph, Jed, and Lon Chaney worked the officers like master puppeteers. By the time the men had eaten, and played one hand of poker, they'd turned into best friends with promises to get together at a well-known watering hole the next evening for beers.

"Before you go," Jed said in the midst of ushering the officers out, "you never did mention why you ended up on my doorstep this morning."

The officers exchanged a pointed glance. "Ah hell," one said, "we may as well tell him."

"Tell me what?" Jed looked the soul of innocence.

"We had a couple of fellows show up at the station house early this morning. They accused you of, well, something that's totally untrue. Worse, they said you were the guiding force behind a massacre up in the San Gabriels last night."

two. Code is so simple, I didn't need to find Gideon to crack it. Just move up the alphabet two letters."

"That's a cheerful note to end on. Maybe there'll be some way to use that information in our favor," Jed said, thoughtfully.

"Lots of anti-cult sentiment floating around," Jon noted with a wry grin.

"Maybe you're onto something." An idea blazed brightly in Blake's head. *"Les and Karl's mate is on the run from a cult that fell into blood sacrifice. There has to be some way to leverage that."*

"I like it," Keir punctuated his words with a growl. *"If we could get the public to see Hunters as just one more blood-crazed cult, we'd be in excellent shape."*

"If all of us work on it, we can make it happen." Jon smiled, a rare enough event that Blake almost didn't recognize the mountain cats' alpha.

Jed reverted to normal speech. "That's a task for tomorrow, once we're all better rested and can strategize. Who's for poker?"

"Me." Blake gave Jed a shove toward the door. "I've always wanted to fleece you for a few thousand."

"Easy words," Jed countered. "I'm going to make you eat them."

Blake broke out laughing. The others joined in as they trooped down the hall and into the great room.

"Tell me," Adolph demanded. "I am always up for a good joke."

"Blake said he was going to make a poor man out of me," Jed rolled his eyes.

Adolph glanced at Blake. "You will be in for an uphill battle, my man. Jed's balls are made of gold."

"My gold balls are bigger than his," Blake retorted, and everyone in the room broke into gales of laughter.

He gave Sophie a quick kiss as he passed by where she and the other women had settled near the grand piano. "We'll go home soon."

She kissed him back before placing her mouth near his ear. "I can hardly wait."

Sophie lounged between her mates as the car passed through Barstow on its way to Las Vegas. They'd remained at Jed's for two more days without so much as a hint of trouble from the authorities. Their party with the two officers and their wives had been so much fun, Jed made a date to do it again the following week. The beginnings of a plan to discredit Hunters, drag them into the public eye, and label them as one more crazed cult, was in play. The men were excited about it, but so was Megan, who had ample reason to fear and hate cults from her Garden of Eden experience.

"How much farther to your house?" Sophie asked.

"It's *our* house," Gideon corrected her.

"Maybe another couple hours," Blake said.

"We got lucky the way things worked out," she commented.

"Not so much luck." Blake looked sidelong at her from where he sat behind the wheel. "Jed's a brilliant tactician. Things might not have looked so rosy if Lon Chaney Jr. and Adolph Zukor weren't there vouching for us."

"Regardless." Sophie was determined to put a positive spin on things. "I'm just grateful you're not in jail."

"Be grateful we weren't detained in California to answer questions, either," Mac said from the backseat. "That could've been awkward."

"I spent some time talking with Jed and the other alphas," Blake said. "We're going to hang back, see which way the winds blow in D.C. while we activate our plan to annihilate Hunters. If there's enough positive sentiment in the Capitol, we'll ride the wave and petition for equal rights."

"But that would expose you." Fear clutched at Sophie, turning her belly into a writhing mass of snakes.

"True, but it would be for the best of causes. They'll never offer us equal rights until they see us as people, just like them," Blake said.

"Hear, hear, boss," Mac jumped in, clapping his hands together.

"None of that will happen for a while." Blake tucked an arm around her. "Try not to worry. Besides, we have your gift to fall back on. We can test the waters that way and not make our move until things look certain for us."

Breath whooshed from her. "Yes. Of course I can do that. And I will." She placed a hand on Blake's thigh. "You are not going anywhere until I deem it safe."

The corners of his mouth twitched. "Our mate has spoken."

"Don't make fun of me."

"He's not," Mac said. "But we love it when you go all fierce on us."

She dozed off and on until they turned onto a side road off the main highway. The bumps and ruts of the dirt track filled her with excitement because it meant they were almost home. She hadn't had a real home—ever. Life on the res was at the white man's behest. They could force Indians to move whenever they wanted.

"You don't live in Las Vegas?" she asked her mates.

"No. We're about ten miles north of town next to a year-round artesian well. It ensures we'll always have water, despite being in the desert," Gideon replied.

"Not much farther now," Blake said. "If you squint and look real hard, you can see the house on the horizon."

Sophie peered through the dust-caked windscreen, and her mouth fell open. "That?" She pointed.

"Yes, but you can't see it very well yet," Gideon said.

"Wow! It looks bigger than Jed's place," she murmured.

"Different architectural style," Mac pointed out. "It's one story, with a bunch of outbuildings for the cars and the shop and other things we want to keep out of the weather."

The car glided closer, and palms came into view as well as a stone wall surrounding the property. Giant saguaro cacti and Joshua trees grew thickly inside the wall. The house was built of plaster and wood. A sprawling structure with beige walls and lots of windows, it blended in with the surrounding desert. She felt magic flow from Blake and tall gates opened for their car, closing once they drove through.

Excitement spilled through her. She craned her neck, looking everywhere. "I want to see it all at once." She laughed. "Guess I need to slow down."

Blake brought the car to a stop at the head of a circular driveway. Unlike the dirt road leading to the house, the driveway was paved with pink and green crushed stones that glittered in the late day sun.

Gideon pushed the car door open and got out, offering her a hand. She stepped into sun-dappled shade from the many plants growing nearby. It smelled heavenly, like the desert, but filled with the piquant scent of greenery too. She inhaled deeply. "This sounds hokey, but even the air smells alive."

"It's our magic." Blake walked to where she stood. "It surrounds the house and protects it when we're gone."

"Keeps others out too." Mac exited the backseat. "They can't even see the place, if they happened to stumble across it, which isn't likely."

"Is it a private road?" she asked, gazing through the gate that Mac was pulling closed.

"Yup." Blake took her hand. "Only place it leads to is here."

"What do you want to see first?" Gideon asked. "The grounds or the inside?"

"How about a quick tour out here, and then inside?" she answered. Her heart was full as she took everything in. She'd always loved the desert. It had been her only true home while she lived on the reservation. To be able to live in her favorite setting—with a luxurious home as a bonus—stole her breath and filled her with happiness.

"Sure. Won't take long." Blake tugged on her hand, and she fell into step next to him. "This is the garage. We all love cars, so it's pretty full. The building next to it—" he pointed "—is the shop. The one behind that is the pump house. Keeps the well from freezing on the rare days it gets truly cold."

"How about those little houses over there?" She extended an arm toward two structures that looked like large versions of doll houses.

"Guest quarters for when we have company." Blake laughed and the sound warmed her. "It's not a common occurrence, but other shifters do stay with us occasionally."

"That's the barn," Gideon chimed in. "We could keep horses if you wanted. Or anything else your heart desired."

"Thank you." She grabbed his hand with her free one. "It would depend how much we're here. Animals tie you down."

"Hey!" Mac settled his hands on her shoulders from behind. "I feel left out. You need an extra hand to hang onto me too."

"That's our cue to go inside." Blake led them around to the front door. Another quick hit of power, and the door sprang open.

"Guess you don't believe in locks." Sophie glanced his way.

"Magic is better," he said. "Cleaner and easier. We'll teach you the frequency to get in and out. Locks can be picked, but no one can defeat magic—unless they have power stronger than ours."

His words cast a pall over her joy. "Hunters." She spat the word, but it still made her feel dirty. "Have they ever been here?"

"No. Never," Mac said. "Besides our power trumps theirs—unless they cheat like they did ganging up on Jed."

"We aim to keep Hunters away from this place," Blake said, sounding stern.

"You got that right," Gideon growled. "No Hunter talk or thoughts. Not today."

"It's a special day," Mac concurred. "The day we're bringing our mate home."

Blake met Sophie's gaze with his aquamarine eyes. "We could take turns carrying you across the threshold."

"Nah." Mac lifted his hands from her shoulders and motioned to Blake. "You're the alpha. You do the honors for our mate."

Blake scooped her up as if she were weightless, and she nestled into his arms as he mounted three broad, shallow flagstone steps and carried her into her new home. "Before I put you down," he said, "we're heading into Vegas soon. I want to make things legal, marry you."

Sophie felt the quick bite of tears. Words wouldn't come, so she just nodded against his chest.

"While we're there, we'll buy you what you need," Gideon said.

"Alice was kind enough to give you some of her clothes," Mac added, "but we want you to have things of your own."

Blake settled her on her feet. Before she focused on the house, she turned to her mates. "Having all of you for my very own is plenty. I've never needed things."

Emotion played over the men's striking features. "Sure and that may well be the nicest thing anyone's ever said to me," Mac crooned, his brogue thicker than ever.

"Took the words right out of my mouth," Blake said.

"Are you ready to see your new home?" Gideon asked.

Sophie nodded. "Make the bedroom last, please."

Blake angled a brow. "Afraid we'll get stuck there and not leave for a while?"

"Exactly." Sophie smothered a self-conscious smile and followed her mates as they walked her through acres of living area, studies, a room with a billiards table, and even a studio with a projector to play movies. The floors were beautifully toned slate interspersed with shiny marble, and the rooms large. All the living areas flowed into one another. Glass and wood blended with the stone into a delightfully artistic mixture. The house sported two kitchens, one partially submerged in the cool desert ground.

"For when it's high summer," Blake explained.

"That way the heat from cooking doesn't raise the temperature in the rest of the house," Gideon said.

"I want to show you our rooms, but then I'd like us to go back outside," Blake said. "There's a special garden a short distance from the house. If you approve, I'd like it to be the place we welcome you as our mate."

"I'd love to see it."

"Good. This is Mac's room. Gideon's is here, and mine is at the end of the hall."

He opened doors and she gazed into each man's bedroom. They were unique to her mates. Gideon's was filled with sculptures and paintings, Mac's with elaborate wood carvings, and Blake's was lined with overflowing bookshelves.

Sophie stopped in the doorway of Blake's room. "What did each of you do?"

"You mean when we still had to work?" Mac inquired with a lifted brow. At her nod, he grinned. "I was an archaeologist. Even taught at the University in Dublin until it became impossible to hide the fact I wasn't growing older."

"I'm an artist." Gideon bent and kissed her cheek. "All the things in my room are my work, plus many of my pieces are scattered in museums around the world. I ran into the same problem as Mac. Most of the art world believes I'm dead, and that's how it shall remain."

Sophie focused on Blake.

"I'm an architect."

"You designed this house," she guessed.

"Yes, this one and others. I actually played a role in figuring out Jed's too. It was an odd piece of property and needed a lot of work to support a structure the size of his." Blake extended an arm. "Come on, darling. We can talk vocations later."

Magic tinged with lust rose from him and her other two mates. Their combined sensuality was contagious, and suddenly it seemed like forever since they'd brought each other off in the car during the trip from Los Angeles. She tucked a hand beneath Blake's arm and walked next to him through one of the home's many side doors.

Light was fading from the sky, but the earth and stones still held some of the day's warmth. Blake led her to the top of a knoll overgrown with shrubs near the back of the property. A well-used path wound downward from it.

She heard water before she saw it. Two more twists down the trail brought them to a small sandy area next to a fast running stream bubbling up from somewhere below them. Pink sandstone lined the creek's walls, and the music of birds and insects filled her ears.

"Go ahead," Blake urged. "Touch the water. This part of the artesian system is geothermal. It's warm."

Sophie knelt and dipped her hand into the stream. "Not just warm, delightful," she pronounced.

Mac and Gideon scrambled after them and began slithering out of their clothes. "There's a perfect pool right here," Mac called over one shoulder as he waded into the water. Gideon followed him and they settled on the bottom of the pool. Water reached their shoulders. Through its clear surface, she saw their cocks swell, hard and inviting.

Blake closed his arms around her from behind, his erection prodding her back. "Want me to help you out of those clothes?" The catch in his voice betrayed his excitement even more than his ridged flesh.

She hip butted his groin before twisting to face him. "How about this?" Sophie unbuttoned her top and tossed it over a nearby bush. She'd lost her bra somewhere in the car when they were driving.

Blake groaned and bent to take a nipple into his mouth while he twirled the other one between his fingers. Hunger spilled through her and she grappled for his cock, holding onto it through his trousers while she worked on undoing the buttons holding his pants in place on his slender hips. They pooled around his feet, and he made a frantic, very male noise as she closed her hands around his cock, skin to skin.

"We want you too, sweetheart," Mac called from the water.

"There's an awesome flat rock you could lean over," Gideon suggested with a familiar lewd undertone in his words that always got her even hotter.

Blake let go of her breasts. "Go on into the water," he told her. "I've got to untangle my shoes from my pants."

"I can help you with that." Breath burned her throat as arousal took her by storm. She knelt, meaning to unlace his shoes, but somehow his cock ended up in her mouth on the way down. She worked him hard with her hand and sucked up and down his shaft, grazing her teeth along the head of his penis.

His cock grew stiffer in her mouth, and she reached a hand between his legs, pressing on the magic spot just behind his balls. Blake cried out, making the guttural sounds that always presaged orgasm. His cock spasmed, and she worked him harder, not backing off until he quieted.

He dragged himself from her mouth. "Gideon and Mac need you," he managed between pants.

"I never did get to your shoes."

"He can get his own damn shoes," Mac called. "Get over here, wench, I'm about to spend from jacking myself."

"Watching you and Blake got us hotter than pistols," Gideon said. "Besides," he added slyly, "you haven't come yet. Get in here, sweetheart."

"Let us take care of you," Mac chimed in.

"Watch out for those silver-tongued devils," Blake teased and gave her a gentle push toward the water.

She unbuttoned her skirt and stepped out of it where it fell around her feet. Next she bent to unlace her stout boots. They were the only shoes she had, but clothes didn't matter. Not right now. The only thing that did was closing the distance between herself and her other two mates.

Sophie waded into deliciously warm water. Bath temperature, it licked at her, increasing her arousal as it surrounded the inflamed nub between her legs. The men held out their arms invitingly.

"Straddle me, darling." Mac rubbed his penis. "Gideon will take you from behind."

Surging forward, she felt him steady her waist with both hands. Sophie wrapped fingers around his waiting cock and lowered herself onto it with Mac's help. The buoyancy of the water added another dimension to their lovemaking.

Gideon knelt behind her and teased her anus with his fingers. When she squirmed toward him, wanting more, he replaced his fingers with his cock, sliding it in inch by inch. Mac wove his arms beneath hers and crushed her to him just before his mouth found hers and he buried his tongue in it. Where her nipples pressed against his chest, sensation blazed through her.

She rocked between their two cocks as lust tracked from her feet to the top of her head, taking her higher and higher. This was a familiar game they played, walking along passion's razor edge without falling off it into climax. She felt Blake's energy join in, felt his still hard cock drive into her side. Breaking away from Mac's mouth, she kissed Blake long and deep.

The men fucked her harder, faster. Someone reached for her clit, and the game was up. Orgasm roared from her, shaking her to her core. She felt the men judder hard, releasing in pussy and anus, and she reached for Blake's cock, holding tight.

When she could talk, she slid her hand up his shaft. "Do you want to come again?"

He nodded. "With you, I want to come forever, but it can wait."

Gideon pulled out of her body, and Mac lifted her off him. Warm water rushed in, laving her, and she ducked to her shoulders before straightening.

Tenderness streamed from her mates. She saw it in their eyes and felt it in the magic simmering in the air around them. Night had fallen while they made love, but the sandstone glowed, reflecting light from the rising moon.

Blake wrapped his arms around her. "Will you run with us, Sophie? Not for long and not very far, but my coyote would be honored if you'd howl at the moon with us."

"It's safe enough," Gideon said. "Plenty of wild coyotes roam the desert."

"We're the only people out here," Mac said. "There used to be a mining camp, but it closed up ten years back."

"I don't need you to convince me." Love for her mates coursed through her, turning her world magical. "I used to howl at the moon all by myself. I'd love to run with you. Let me dry off and put my clothes and boots back on."

The men shifted while she slipped back into her things. It was cooling fast. While running naked held an appeal, she'd chill down quickly. The coyotes milled around her, nudging, and licking, and she petted them shamelessly, digging deep into their rough pelts and raining kisses on their shiny, black noses.

"Ready?" Blake's voice rang in her mind.

"You bet! Don't go too fast, you'll lose me." She stood.

"You're our mate, we'll never lose you." Gideon nosed her one last time before taking off up the trail they'd followed to the hot spring.

She followed her mates as the moon rose higher in the sky. They slipped through the fence, while someone's magic opened a gate for her. On a rise a quarter mile from the house, the coyotes formed a ring around her, raised their muzzles skyward and broke into a cacophony of yips and howls.

Sophie canted her head back and yipped right along with them. A group of wild coyotes ran up and joined their song. They nuzzled Sophie as if she was one of them, and she reached into their minds with her magic wishing them good hunting and many pups.

It felt so right, and so complete, she knew she was home. Her home. Her mates. Her place in the universe. All the aching desperation of her earlier life fell away. In a backhanded way, Abe had finally done her a favor. If she hadn't been so frantic to make certain he was dead, she'd never have followed him into the Palisades, never met Jed…

"And then you'd never have met us," Blake finished her thought, having been in her mind.

Perhaps sensitive to the magic Blake expended in telepathy, the wild coyotes galloped off and began howling again a little farther east.

"I love all of you. Thank you for believing in me and wanting me for your mate."

Light flashed around her as the men found their human bodies and surrounded her with their heat and love.

"Let's get you home," Blake said.

"Us too." Gideon shivered. "The temperature is perfect for my coyote, but chilly when I'm a man." He took off at a quick clip with everyone pacing him. Inside the gate, she turned and stopped before they entered the house and tossed one last yipping howl at the moon.

"The mate bond never lies." Blake broke into a belly laugh. "Her last name might be Laughing Wolf, but she's a coyote beneath that human skin."

"If she wasn't before she mated with us, she sure is now." Mac laughed too, and all of them ducked inside through a door Blake held open.

"What'll it be?" Blake asked. "A midnight supper or another round of loving?"

"Both?" Sophie looked from one man to the next, batting her eyes disingenuously. "Since the three of you are naked, the logical order would be—"

Blake crushed his mouth over hers, effectively silencing her, and Mac and Gideon surrounded her with their bodies.

Cradled between her mates, love and need spilled through her. Sophie sent a silent prayer spinning outward that she'd always be worthy of their love.

"We feel the same way, darling," Gideon murmured near her ear.

"We waited a long time for you, princess." Mac tickled her other ear with his tongue.

Blake raised his mouth from hers. "We're well mated, Sophie our heart, our love. Enough talking, unless it's to ask for hands or mouth or other body parts."

"Aye, aye, boss." Gideon clapped Blake on the back.

"Whose bed?" Mac asked.

"Since you asked, we'll use yours." Blake scooped her off her feet and carried her down the hall with the others right behind them.

This is the end of *Sophie's Shifters*, but not the end of the Wolf Clan

Shifter Series. The next book only exists in my mind's eye at the moment, but I'm pretty sure Jon and his lieutenants will find their mate. If you enjoy my shifter stories, you might like *Underground Heat,* a boxed set of three complete paranormal romance novels. Also sold individually. A sample follows.

ABOUT THE AUTHOR

Ann Gimpel is a national bestselling author. A lifelong aficionado of the unusual, she began writing speculative fiction a few years ago. Since then her short fiction has appeared in a number of webzines and anthologies. Her longer books run the gamut from urban fantasy to paranormal romance. Once upon a time, she nurtured clients. Now she nurtures dark, gritty fantasy stories that push hard against reality. When she's not writing, she's in the backcountry getting down and dirty with her camera. She's published over 50 books to date, with several more planned for 2018 and beyond. A husband, grown children, grandchildren, and wolf hybrids round out her family.

Keep up with her at www.anngimpel.com or http://anngimpel.blogspot.com

If you enjoyed what you read, get in line for special offers and pre-release special reads. Sign up for Ann's newsletter on her website or her blog.

SAMPLE FROM ROMAN'S GOLD

...Devon Heartshorn strode past the pale blue Victorian. He'd watched Kate Roman run up the steps and let herself inside. He was nearly certain she knew she was being followed, but she'd played it very cool. Even though he hadn't been able to see her once the door was shut, his genetically-enhanced senses told him she'd been just inside, watching him.

He surreptitiously rearranged himself. Just following Kate had been immensely arousing. He'd known she worked as a sex surrogate, but he hadn't counted on her sheer animal magnetism or the hot swing of her hips. She was maybe five feet eight with curves to spare. Full breasts pushed against the front of her denim jacket. He'd gotten a good look when she'd been at right angles to him running up her office steps. Tight jeans displayed a generous butt.

It wasn't just her lush figure and the bright hair peeking out from under her scarf that heated his blood. The way she walked practically screamed she owned the street. She had presence, an almost regal bearing. Though she hadn't turned around, he knew from pictures that her eyes were amber, shading to golden. Cat eyes. Just like the cat she was.

She was magnificent. He didn't think he'd be able to capture her. It would be a crime to put something that perfect behind bars. He shook his head. Dark hair fell into his face. He pushed it aside and ducked into a coffee shop. Everything was self-serve. He held his wrist computer up to the auto teller, ordered ten credits worth of food, and scanned his personal ID. The auto teller obligingly gave him a code, which popped up on his screen. Devon marched down the aisle. When he saw something he wanted, he scanned the barcode on his display, a glass door opened, and he took his item.

Coffee and pastry in hand, he sat at a table and raked his fingers through his hair. He wasn't pleased about his current assignment, but he didn't see any way out of it. He'd moved from the Mojave Desert three months ago to take a job as a lieutenant with the City of Berkeley Police Department. He'd even gone through the series of infusions to alter his already-enhanced genetics, so he'd be more sensitive to shifters. The last one had been three days ago, and his arm still ached. Something in the IV fluid was a hell of an irritant. He was glad to be done with that part of things.

His jaw tightened. Law enforcement had changed dramatically since he'd finished his criminal justice degree at UCLA. Devon had planned to go to law school, but first he'd needed to figure out a way to pay for it. Half Paiute from his father's side, he'd applied to the Tribal Consortium for an educational loan. Because he wasn't a full blood, they'd turned him down, and he'd ended up signing on as an officer with the San Bernardino County Sheriff's office.

A failed marriage and an underwater mortgage deep-sixed his law school plans. Fifteen years later, he was still working as a police officer. It wasn't such a bad life—until the governmental directive to round up shifters was signed into law two years ago.

A familiar pain knifed through him. His mother had been half-shifter; mixed genetics had cost her life. He'd petitioned the parole board to free her, had promised to keep a close eye on her. His request was denied.

"If we do it for her," the head of the board told him, "well, son, we'd have to do it for everybody's mother. I'm sure you understand."

Devon hadn't understood, though. The push to rid the United States of shifters made no sense to him. There may have been a few that used their animal forms to harm humans, but human criminals harmed humans too. His mother wasn't a threat to anyone. Not then, not ever. Her health had never been good, and she'd died in prison from a lung ailment, probably pneumonia.

Devon had visited her regularly. Even prisoners had rights and couldn't be denied visitors unless they acted out badly. His mother was far too ill to do anything but lay on her thin prison mattress, coughing. She'd told him not to grieve for her, but he couldn't help it. She'd only been fifty-seven. At the funeral, his two sisters and father hadn't said two words to him. He was a living, breathing representation of the ruling class, the reason his mother wasn't with them anymore.

He looked at his half empty cup of coffee and barely touched pastry, and his stomach knotted. He didn't feel hungry anymore. He'd wanted to talk with his family after his mother's death. After all, it wasn't like he'd been the one to round her up and stick her in that women's prison in Chino.

But I didn't do anything to help her, either. Guilt shriveled his soul. He'd given up after the parole board turned him down the second time.

Devon winced. He'd done his share of trapping shifters and seeing them imprisoned. Once the governmental directive had come down removing their human rights, he'd taken his responsibilities as a sworn law enforcement officer seriously. It didn't matter how he felt. He was bound by oath to uphold the law.

What about protect? the same inner voice nagged. *Aren't I supposed to protect the innocent?*

His mother had been one of the sweetest, kindest women he'd ever known. And now she was dead. Because of her blood. His hands fisted by his sides. He shot to his feet, almost tipping the flimsy table over, and stormed out of the restaurant. Blinded by guilt and rage, he ran square into a couple coming in.

"Watch it, dude," the man growled.

"Sorry." Devon stumbled to the side.

Outside the café, he walked fast, but it wasn't enough to assuage his guilt, so he broke into a run to ease the pain in his guts. He ran until the city limit sign flashed past and kept on going. He was off duty. No one expected him anywhere. If he went back to the station, they'd just grill him about Kate, and he'd have to fill out a report. Maybe he'd tell them he hadn't been able to find her. That might buy her a few more days of freedom.

He drew up hard and bent over, hands on his knees, sucking air. He'd never reneged on his duty before. He couldn't believe he'd even considered such a thing. If his superiors found out, he'd never work in law enforcement again. He might even get tossed in jail.

Yeah, just like Mom. Maybe it's what I deserve...

Devon worked his long hair into a single braid to get it out of his face, and then took off at a fast jog. Maybe if he ran long enough, the remorse sluicing through him would ease. He'd read the official paperwork condemning shifters—all of it. It hadn't made a whole lot of sense. After all, he had shifter blood, just not enough to change into anything. The rules were quite clear, though. Fifty percent was the dividing line. No one bothered to hide their shifter background. It was right on their birth certificates, so hunting them had been easy. Too easy, at least until some shifter organization had taken to wiping databases. He'd asked to be reassigned after his mother's death, but his desk captain laughed and told him to grow a thicker hide.

Shunned by his fellow officers for being soft-hearted, shunned by his family for his mother's demise, Devon finally couldn't stand it anymore. He had to leave the Mojave Desert with its painful memories. It had taken a while to find another job, but the City of Berkeley finally offered him an out. They had a new hush-hush task force. He'd only found out he'd be tracking shifters after he'd accepted the job, moved, and been sworn in.

The slap of his shoes against asphalt boomed loud in his ears. Sweat ran down his sides. Hovercraft whirred overhead. The sky was thick with them outside the city limits. His throat stung. It didn't take much to erode the already-marginal air quality. A craft flew too low. Devon was certain it was in violation of the hundred-foot minimum, but didn't radio in the infraction. Why should he? His jurisdiction ended at the city limit sign.

"Hey, handsome. What you running away from? Got an angry woman on your tail?"

He whipped around. A young Asian, probably Vietnamese from the look of her fair skin and high cheekbones, smiled. He came to a stop, momentarily confused, and then smacked the palm of his hand against his head. Of course. Hookers weren't allowed inside the city limits, but many women set up shop close enough to Berkeley's edge to lure clients. Maybe a diversion was just the thing he needed.

"Nope. Just running." He smiled back.

She sashayed over to him, hips swinging. Her sarong gave him a fair view of the tops of her high, firm breasts. "It's been pretty slow today. You're quite a cutie. I'd be willing to give you a deal."

He quirked a brow, heart still pounding from his run. "What kind of deal?"

"Depends what you want." She tugged the low neck of her dragon-patterned, red and black dress aside, offering him a quick peek at a brown nipple....